STARLIGHT
A FANTASY CHRISTMAS ANTHOLOGY

THE SCREAMING PEN

Cover: Adrijana Cernic

Edited: Adryanna Monteiro

Format: A. A. Warne

Publisher: The Screaming Pen

To the dreamers…
The ones who dream of beautiful times,
that create the energy of Christmas,
a happy home,
a fun community,
…you make the world a wonderful place to live in.

To those who live…
The ones who live the dream,
bringing energy to life,
creating homes and communities,
in the way you know best,
…you make the world a wonderful place to live in.

INTRODUCTION

There's an interesting thing that goes on inside an author's head. Swirls of ideas, flickers of imagery, waves of emotions — and at the same time, all of our senses are engaged.

It's never about where we get our ideas from, but rather the struggle to get them down on paper — there's too many! Even if we tried, our brains get excited and our imaginations kick up a gear, forcing our poor fingers to race across the keyboard to keep up.

Then, on the off chance, we move away from our quiet and isolated little writing spaces and meet other authors.

This is where the fun really begins — ideas become plans, plans become written pages, which in turn become the very pages of our books.

But first, it always starts with the idea. For this book, it's Starlight.

As you go from one story to the next, you'll notice that sometimes the theme is obvious, and other times, it's hidden like an Easter Egg. There are no rules in the writing world — these characters pull us along and are clear on how we tell their stories.

So buckle up in your comfy seat with your delicious drink, because ten fantastical worlds await.

I introduce to you:
STARLIGHT: A Fantasy Christmas

Happy reading,
~ Amanda Warne

MARIA AND THE MOUSE, KING

DRAGONNESS WYVERNA

M aria Stahlbaum lived in December Twenty-Fourth, which is as close to Christmas as you could live without being a Claus. Christmas itself could be seen from her bedroom window, the gingerbread houses bathed in the light of the Christmas star. The gumdrop lights cast bright colors across the snow, the royal icing filled the air with intoxicating sweetness, and the sugar-glass panes showed the trees glowing in the highly decorated parlors. Sugar cookies decorated like snowmen were set out by the fireplace in a nearby house, and her stomach growled. She licked her lips, only to be drawn out of her hungry reverie by tiny claws crawling up the puffed sleeves of her pinafore, as a little, furry body hid behind her black curls.

Maria turned her coal-black eyes to the bright red eyes of her little friend, and she tapped on the sugar-glass of her own window. "Do you see it, King? Doesn't it look beautiful?"

The black mouse wiggled his nose, his tail curling around Maria's neck as he peered through the window. "I see it: overly sweet and full of itself. Typical Christmas."

Maria tapped his nose gently in rebuke. "Don't say that. The elves might hear."

King sat on his hind paws and began to clean his whiskers. "The elves are downstairs playing in the powdered sugar. They'll be on a sugar high all night."

She shuddered, envisioning the little creatures running rampant through the house. "Mother Gigone won't be happy about that. I'm glad we're going to Christmas tonight and won't have to watch that carnage."

"Clara is dancing tonight, isn't she?"

"And Fritz is joining the Nutcracker Corps. It's a big night for both of them." Maria's reflection came into focus, and she couldn't help but compare herself to her siblings. Fritz and Clara were both blonde, pale, and wouldn't look out of place on the top of a Christmas tree. Her black hair, black eyes, and plump cheeks weren't the cherubic Christmas standard that her brother and sister met, and despite how hard she practiced, she couldn't replicate their effortless grace at the barre. She turned away from the window and smoothed down her red pinafore, trying to look presentable.

"Maria!" Clara called from the hall. "Make sure you have your shoes on! We're leaving in five minutes!"

Maria made a face and went to her wardrobe to fetch her stockings and shoes. "I hate these things," she complained, sitting on her bed. "There are so many buttons!"

"Better than those ballet slippers Clara wears," King squeaked.

"True." Maria paused, listening for the door, then she slipped her foot into the boot and ran her fingers up the buttons. They popped into their holes easily, and much faster than if she'd done it by hand. Her fingers tingled with the magic as she grabbed the second boot.

"What are you doing?"

Maria jumped at her sister's shrill voice, falling back onto her quilt in alarm. Clara, her blond, willowy, perfect sister stood in the doorway, dressed in the glittering white of a snow fairy. Before Maria could recover, Clara spotted King and screamed. The mouse scurried off the table, but Clara was already throwing things.

"Get away!" she shrieked. "Get away, you horrid little beast!"

"Clara, no!" Maria grabbed her sister's arms.

Shaking her off, Clara reached for a candlestick, but when she looked back at the table, King was gone. "Evil little beast. Did you see its eyes?" She shuddered then turned back to Maria. "Speaking of evil, what were you doing to your boots?"

Maria retreated to the bed. "Nothing. I was just buttoning them, that's all."

"If you keep lying, you'll end up on the naughty list."

Maria grimaced wordlessly and began to manually button her last boot.

"Using that magic will get you on the naughty list, too."

"I was only buttoning my boots!"

"It's *evil*, Maria. Santa…"

"Santa uses magic on his reindeer. That's how they fly!"

"That's different."

"How?"

"It's Christmas magic from the Christmas star!" Clara pointed at the shining light outside the window. "It's good. It's pure. Your magic… It's something else. And if it's not Christmas magic, it's not nice. It's naughty."

Maria looked at the star shining over Santa's workshop then turned away, guilt gnawing at her. "I don't mean to be naughty. It's a part of me."

"I know." Clara sighed, sitting beside her. "I know you think so, but that magic… That's the kind of magic that the nutcrackers fight against. The thing that Fritz is going to be fighting against." She took her hands. "You don't want to be like one of those monsters in Halloween, do you?"

Maria shook her head. "No."

Clara patted her hand. "Good. Now, finish buttoning your shoes, and we can go to Christmas and watch Fritz become a nutcracker."

Maria managed to smile while she wrestled with her final button. "I'm very proud of him."

"And you should be. He's worked very hard." She took Maria's boot, finishing the buttons for her. "You know, if you tried…"

"I do try!"

"Then you need to try harder. You need to be jolly. This is Christmas Eve, and Godfather Drosselmeyer has a reputation to uphold."

Maria stared at her lap. "I know."

"If you know, then do better." Clara sighed at Maria's dejected expression and stood. "Pouting will also put you on the naughty list. Come now. Our carriage is waiting."

Maria went to her wardrobe to retrieve her cloak and fur muff. She jumped when her fingers found King hiding in her muff, but she was relieved her little friend was coming with her.

Maria followed her sister down the carpeted stairs, ducking as a particularly exuberant elf swung shrieking from the ceiling garland. The elf cackled and dropped to the railing, chasing after her in an attempt to pull her curls. A peppermint cracked into its back, knocking it off the banister, and the elf shrieked in rage before getting distracted by the Christmas tree. Maria peered onto the landing and smiled at her older brother. Fritz grinned back and winked, tucking the slingshot into the breast pocket of his red nutcracker uniform.

Clara tsked. "Aren't you a little old for slingshots, Fritz?"

"Any weapon in a battle," Fritz replied. "That elf was good practice for the ghoulies on the front. Besides, I couldn't let it ruin Maria's hair."

"Thank you, Fritz," Maria chuckled. "But next time, use your sword. That would teach it."

"Maria!" Clara frowned. "That's not very nice!"

"Tell the elf that."

"Leave her alone, Clara," Fritz said, putting an arm around Maria as the trio stepped into the crisp evening. "It's a special night. Let's focus on merriment, family, and presents."

"So long as Maria remembers to stay on the nice list and doesn't embarrass us."

"She won't." Fritz winked at Maria then helped her into the carriage.

Maria settled onto the velvet cushion, stroking King's fur subtly as Fritz and Clara filed in behind her. Their godfather had taken the carriage earlier to help the Clauses prepare the feast, leaving Clara in charge. She took the responsibility seriously, filling the short trip with reminders for Maria on how to behave, where to stand to watch the performance, and when to clap when Fritz was awarded his new rank. Maria nodded after every reminder, but her mind was on the dancing and the sweets that were to come.

The Christmas Feast naturally took place at Santa's house, which sat at the very center of Christmas. It was the tallest and grandest of the Christmas gingerbread houses. The sugar-glass windows were decorated with iced snowflakes, candied wreaths hung on all the grand doors, and royal icing wove itself in ornate, wintery patterns along the walls. The whole effect was like a dream, which was then complimented with the falling snow and the warm smell of sugar cookies wafting from the swinging doors. King shivered in anticipation inside Maria's muff as Fritz helped her from the carriage.

"Remember," Clara hissed, stepping out onto the snow beside her. "Nice, not naughty."

Maria nodded and stepped into line, following her siblings into the grand house. The indoors were just as grand as the outdoors, with every entry lined with garland, mistletoe hanging from the ceiling, at least three trees in every room, and candles on every ledge. It was a veritable wonderland, the poignant scents of fir and pine mingling with the sweet cookie smells she'd noticed earlier.

Clara and Fritz passed their coats to the housekeeper while Maria ducked behind one of the foyer trees, helping King hide in the branches before she surrendered her own coat. King scampered along the garland, following Maria and her siblings into the dancehall. A handsome young man approached Clara the moment she stepped into the room, whisking her onto the dancefloor. Fritz strode after her, asking another young woman to dance. Maria, meanwhile, went to the refreshments table, helping herself to the punch while her siblings danced.

The dancers created a grand spectacle, gliding along to the crooning of the flutes and violins, the sharp staccato of the piccolo accenting the steps perfectly. Clara stayed in the middle of the dancefloor, spinning from partner to partner, her movements lithe and graceful, a perfect snowflake on the arms of her partners. Maria moved closer to the wall where King was hiding, subtly passing him a cranberry as they admired her sister's grace.

This was Clara's dream, to rise to the top of the Nice List and take her place as Sugar Plum Fairy, and she matched the world around her. There was magic as she danced, shining snowflakes drifted at the hem of her skirt, following the *tap tap tap* of her pointe ballet shoes. Yes, this was where Clara belonged, but as Maria sipped at her punch, she had the sudden realization that her own black hair and black eyes didn't quite belong amidst the red and green. The thought turned her stomach, and she quickly set the punch down before she grew sick.

After the flow of guests ebbed, Santa made his appearance. His jolly laugh barreled through the orchestration, drawing the attention of the dancers. "Welcome, one and all, to my Christmas feast! I see that Fezziwig has the party already in hand, so I won't disrupt it much further. I only wish to welcome our extra special guests, Nutcracker General Drosselmeyer and his wards, Clara and Fritz Stahlbaum. Young Fritz joins our Nutcracker ranks today, while his sister, Clara, rises to join those most beautiful of creatures, the Sugar Plum Fairies."

There was polite and proud applause, to which Fritz bowed and Clara curtsied, her smile ever so delicate and charming.

Santa continued. "There is a fourth special guest tonight, and he…"

A chill fog spilled into the room, temporarily dimming the bright cheer of the party. A young man entered in the midst of the fog, shrouded in a snow-white fur cloak. He lowered the hood with long, delicate fingers, revealing a face sharp and pale as ice. His piercing blue gaze roamed the dance hall, his expression more chilling than the fog. The guests tensed, their own motley gazes fixed on the newcomer. The mood of the party froze for a long minute, until the newcomer smiled and the ice cracked, letting the cheeriness of a bright, snowy day shine through.

Santa laughed and threw a friendly arm around the newcomer. "There he is! Making an entrance as always." He chortled and waved a broad hand toward the assembly. "May I present Jack Frost, a potential ally in this eternal war to protect Christmas. Do make sure to welcome our new friend thoroughly and show him the goodwill our beloved holiday is known for."

There was more polite applause, then, seeing that Santa had finished his speech, several guests moved to greet Jack. He accepted their welcomes smoothly, his white hair glinting like melting snow in the firelight.

Maria leaned against the wall. "Another ally," she said softly to King. "I wonder what for. I thought we were winning. Still, anything to make Fritz safer."

"*Potential* ally," King corrected.

"Yes, of course, but who wouldn't want to defend Christmas?"

"You'd be surprised," a cool voice replied.

Maria jumped and whirled to see Jack Frost standing in front of her. He had shed his white cloak, revealing a strange, loose, blue tunic that was belted at his hips. His pants were a silver-gray, the tips fringed with frost, and his feet were bare. Maria couldn't help but stare.

Jack grinned. "Shoes have their benefits, but sometimes it's more fun to go without. Wouldn't you agree, Maria?"

"You know me?"

"Your brother was telling me about you," Jack replied, nodding to where Fritz was once again dancing. "He's very fond of you, though your sister seems to think you're headed for the naughty list." His smile widened.

Maria ducked her head. "I try to be nice, but sometimes…"

"Sometimes the pressure of Christmas is too much?"

Maria nodded. "It doesn't seem like I can do anything right. I can't dance, eggnog makes me sick, and…"

"And you have a pet mouse." Jack crouched to get a better look at King. "With red eyes, too. Spooky. What's his name?"

"King. And he can speak for himself."

"Can he? Is he your familiar?" Before Maria could sputter a question, Jack held his finger out to the mouse. "It's a pleasure to meet you, Sir King."

King sat up on his hind legs and placed his little front paws on the man's fingers reverently. "It's always a pleasure to meet someone who doesn't try to kill me."

Jack laughed then held his hand out to Maria. "May I have this dance?"

"I'm not a good dancer."

"Who says you have to be good to dance?"

Several names came to mind, Clara's included, but Jack waggled his fingers. "Come on. It will be fun."

After another moment of hesitation, she accepted his hand and let him pull her onto the dancefloor. She frowned at her own feet, concentrating on the proper steps for a waltz. Jack laughed.

"Don't worry about the steps," he told her. "Focus on me."

Maria forced herself to meet his eyes. She could feel his cold hand on her waist, his cold fingers curling around hers, but it wasn't uncomfortable. In fact, his chill offset the nearly oppressive warmth of the party around them.

"So, who wouldn't want to protect Christmas?" she whispered. "It's the best holiday, all about giving and kindness and love."

"Only those who live in Christmas receive that kindness and love," he replied just as quietly. "Those that live in other holidays receive no such mercy."

Maria's eyes widened. "No. No, that's not true."

"Isn't it?" He cocked his head. "You hear about this so called 'war on Christmas,' but have you ever asked who started the war?"

Maria went silent, unable to answer.

Jack took pity on her discomfort and led her back to the punch bowl, filling her another glass as the trumpets sounded, announcing the start of the Dance of the Sugar Plum Fairy.

Dancers in gilded tutus and leotards spun onto the floor, hair pinned up in neat buns and decorated with tiaras and ribbons. They moved in perfect synchronization, their feet brushing against the floor in a *frappe* before turning in a *pique tour*. Maria recognized all the movements, having seen Clara practice them again and again for hours on end at the barre, and then she saw her sister herself, dancing to center stage with a *petit saut*. The other dancers moved, backfilling in the background as Clara performed her variation to the tinkling of the piccolo. Maria felt her chest swell with pride as she watched her sister, who easily put all other dancers to shame.

When the dance finally ended, everyone assembled clapped in absolute pleasure, and Maria repressed her urge to cheer. Clara beamed with pride, accepting flowers from Mother Gigone as Mrs. Claus topped her hair with a new tiara, one that marked her as a Sugar Plum Fairy.

The dancers parted as Drosselmeyer led Fritz to the Christmas tree, letting him stand before Santa.

Jack stiffened. "Your brother is to be a nutcracker?"

"Yes! He's worked very hard, and we're all proud of him. It's a good thing." She glanced at his darkening expression. "Isn't it?"

"They want you to think it is," he said.

Maria glanced back toward her brother, only half-listening to her godfather as he began to cite Fritz's accomplishments. "What do you mean?"

"A nutcracker is a weapon used on the lines between Halloween and Christmas. Drosselmeyer makes them by hollowing out a man and turning their skin to iron. They can no longer feel, no longer think for themselves. They can only do what Drosselmeyer tells them."

"What?"

He met her gaze, the ice-blue of his eyes flashing with anger. "Christmas magic at its finest."

Maria's mind was reeling. Christmas magic was nice; it couldn't be naughty, it just couldn't! And why should she trust Jack? She didn't know him, but she knew Drosselmeyer. He was the man who had taken her and her siblings into his home, taught them naughty and nice. And he would never hurt Fritz! Not Fritz, who helped her chase away the elves who picked on her, who made her feel like she could be nice. Like she wasn't destined for the Naughty List. Still, something twisted in her gut, her magic warning her that what he said was true. She turned toward the Christmas tree, pushing her way through the crowd.

"Fritz!" She called, trying to warn him as Drosselmeyer raised his hands.

Clara grabbed Maria's arm and yanked her back. "What are you doing?" She hissed. "You're going to ruin everything and end up on the Naughty List!"

"I don't care!" Maria cried. "He's going to hurt him!"

"Godfather Drosselmeyer would never hurt Fritz!"

Even as Clara spoke, Maria's gaze turned to their brother, and she watched in horror as Drosselmeyer put his hands on his shoulders. Fritz's smile froze on his face, then warped, his lips stretching back to reveal his teeth. The crowd clapped as Fritz's warm cheeks turned to cold iron and his red uniform tightened around his chest, shrinking smaller and smaller. Maria saw the moment the cheerful light went out of his eyes, and she charged forward with a wail, grabbing the iron remnant of her brother from the floor.

"Maria!" Drosselmeyer scolded, his single eye turning cold with rage. "What are you doing?"

"Turn him back," Maria demanded, holding up the nutcracker. "Turn him back!"

"Maria," Santa said, his jolly voice strangely threatening as he wagged his finger. "Remember, you'd better not pout."

Clara hurried forward. "Fritz is okay. He's a nutcracker. You knew this was going to happen."

Maria looked at her brother, peering into his gray steel eyes, searching for any sign of life. All she found was her own warped reflection. She hugged him tight. "Oh Fritz, I'm so sorry."

"Maria, give him back," Clara demanded, holding out her hands. "Don't make it any worse for yourself."

Maria lifted her chin, catching sight of Jack moving through the crowd, King on his shoulder. "No. If you're not going to turn my brother back, then I'll find another way."

Santa sighed and turned to Drosselmeyer. "I'm sorry,

Dross, but it looks like your goddaughter has gone on the Naughty List."

As if it were a cue, elves swarmed the floor, weaving around the guests' legs and skirts, wielding tinsel and sharpened candy canes as they charged her. King squeaked in defense, jumping from Jack's shoulder and running to Maria's side, his body puffed as big as it could get as he bared his teeth.

Maria felt her magic start to flow, and she reached for King. Her friend began to grow, hissing and snarling and gnashing his teeth as the elves stumbled in surprise. The once small mouse was now bigger than a reindeer! Fog spilled from Jack's hands, filling the ballroom and hiding them from view as Santa and Drosselmeyer began to shout and the guests began to scream.

Before she knew it, Jack was at Maria's side, lifting her onto King's back. "Run," he told her. "Get your brother out of Christmas. There is other magic out there, magic that can help."

"What magic?" Maria asked desperately.

"Yours." He smiled then pointed. "Once you're out of the city, follow the North star until you can no longer hear the bells. Only then will you be safe."

"You mean the Christmas Star?"

He shook his head. "I mean the North Star. Now, King, go."

King squeaked a confirmation and leapt forward, his tail knocking aside guards that chased after them. Maria yelped and leaned forward, holding her brother in one arm while using the other to hold on for dear life. They broke through the gingerbread doors and raced across the peppermint-cobblestone streets.

Maria looked back only once, and saw Clara standing at the foot of Santa's house, watching them flee with an expression of heartbreak and fury that filled Maria with guilt. Maria quickly turned away, tightening her grip on her nutcracker brother.

"Don't worry, Fritz," she whispered as King crossed Christmas Eve, "I'll take you somewhere Christmas can never touch you." She caught sight of a pale figure lurking in one of the alleyways, one of the Christmas ghosts, and she knew where they could go, where they would be safe.

Halloween.

DRAGONNESS WYVERNA

DW wrote her first story at the age of 8 and hasn't stopped writing since. Her stories primarily feature outcasts and dragons and take place in fantastical worlds woven from imagination.

When she's not writing, she's reading, and when she's not reading, she's playing with her dog, Calcifer.

Follow her on Instagram @the_bookwyrms_bookshelf for colorful book reviews, recommendations, and unboxings!

instagram.com/the_bookwyrms_bookshelf
tiktok.com/@the_bookwyrms_bookshelf

A DRAGON BY STARLIGHT

ADAM GAFFEN

T had to stay calm.

I could do this. After all, I was a post-grad making straight A's at Drake University, the oldest, toughest school in the country.

I was not calm.

In fact, I was so far from calm I couldn't see it with binoculars.

I stomped into the stone building the faculty occupied, which I'd always found charming if odd, and stormed down the hall to my advisor's office.

"Professor!" I shouted, not caring who heard me. This wasn't the time for subtle or discreet.

"Professor!" My voice echoed through the empty corridor. It was late on a Friday afternoon, and I was sure most of my peers and the instructors had all disappeared for the Christmas break. It was just my luck that *this* had happened to me the day before I was supposed to go home.

His office door was closed. No matter. I pounded on it, glass rattling in its frame.

"Professor! You never leave early. I need your help!"

No answer.

Pound! Pound! Pound! Pound!

Still nothing. I tried the handle.

Locked.

The fury I'd been barely bottling burst forth. The white glow around my hand, which I'd masked by wearing my heavy winter gloves, flared, and the handle melted, the heat scorching the wood. The lock disengaged—liquefied—and the door swung inward.

"Oh, shit."

I pushed my way in and called out again with less heat. "Professor?"

His hat and briefcase were in their customary places, and I relaxed. At least he hadn't gone for the day. I fell into my usual seat and dropped my head into my hands. I jerked up, remembering the heat I'd generated, but whatever it was had passed. My hand was normal, encased in the singed remains of the glove.

What happened?

I reviewed the last few days. Maybe I could give Professor Gruffudd something to work with, other than my inexplicable ability to melt metal.

This week I'd had the strangest feeling of being connected to something larger than myself. I'd always been keenly aware of the emotional states of surrounding people. My mom said it was my Welsh ancestors, which didn't explain anything. "Corsen, it's in your blood."

Still didn't make sense, but she wouldn't elaborate.

But I was getting flashes from the students, the professors, everyone I was near. Not thoughts, but feelings. Fear, excitement, anger, joy, lust—the whole gamut. I didn't know what to do, so mostly I ignored it as best I could.

Then came my astronomy lab, my one indulgence. It was an undergrad course, and I had been granted my degrees already, but it was so much fun I talked my way in. It was always my favorite class of the week. Dr. Seryser would dim the lights and take us on a tour of the sky we'd be observing that night. I always lost myself in dreams of the myriad stars and countless possibilities.

Today, we were a few minutes in. Dr. Seryser stopped her lecture. "I've told you many times, no mobiles during class. I know it's the last day before break, but your plans can wait for another forty minutes."

I glanced around in confusion. Who was stupid enough to have forgotten her first rule? Then I realized everyone was looking at me.

Impossible. My cell was in my backpack, as always.

I raised my hands to demonstrate my innocence, but... What?

They were glowing.

Not terribly brightly, no, and I suppose they were easily confused with a phone screen. That didn't change the basic issue. *Hands aren't supposed to glow!*

I panicked. That's my only explanation for what I did next. I stuffed my books into my pack, shoved my arms into my coat, and ran from the room. As I fumbled for gloves, I heard Dr. Seryser's shout of, "Corsen, come back!"

I ignored her.

I don't know why, but my brain kept repeating, "Go to Professor Gruffudd. He'll help."

And now, I was here, with no advisor and no clue what was happening to me.

I sat for probably twenty minutes before he returned. If he was surprised to find me sitting in his locked office, with the door wide open and a puddle of formerly molten metal on the floor, he concealed it well.

"Corsen. I thought I'd see you before break."

His calm tone infuriated me. "You knew?" I half-rose from his seat, but he laid a hand on my shoulder and gently pressed me down.

"You knew?" I repeated.

"It's in your blood, Corsen." He went behind his desk and fiddled with his tea set.

I grumbled, "My mother says that, too. What does it mean?"

"It means you're coming into your inheritance as a dragon shifter."

I shook my head. "What?"

"You, Corsen McAdrich, are descended from dragons. Your family, your extended family, has defended this university for centuries as part of the deal your forebears made to appear human."

"Go back. Dragon shifter? That's a fairy story told to littles. It's not real." I slapped the arm of the chair. "This is real. Your office is real. My degree in astrophysics is real, and so is the internship I have at Jodrell Bank next term. Dragons? Dragon shifters? They aren't."

His smile was entirely too self-assured. "Then explain what happened to my door? Or the light around your arms?"

I glanced down. The glow that had been limited to my hands had spread up my arms, visible through my heavy jumper.

He continued in the same calm voice. "It's called the goleuni'r ddraig, the dragon's glow. It's the sign that your body is ready for its first transformation."

"Stop. This is insane." Dragons? Shifters? I was a scientist, not a creature from a fantasy world. I closed my eyes and leaned back in the chair, trying to make sense of it all.

"Tea?" He held up a steaming cup, and at that instant, nothing in the world sounded more settling than a cuppa. I nodded.

When he finished the rituals and I had a few sips of the brew in me, I felt more ready to confront this lunacy. Maybe I should start with the small stuff.

"Dragons are real. Magic?" Or maybe I'd jump right to the heart of the matter. Why not?

"Oh, yes. Magic is real. More real than science, and far more dangerous."

I thought of the melted doorknob. He might have a point.

"Maybe you ought to start from the beginning."

He offered me a biscuit before answering. "You know nothing of your legacy?"

I shook my head. "Only that my mother said what you did. It's in my blood. But she was talking about being able to feel others' emotions."

He nodded. "That is part of it, yes. It rises earlier than the physical traits, except for your eye and hair colors."

This bit of information fit in well, not that any of it made sense.

"Go on."

"A thousand years ago, when Cymru was independent, Gruffydd ap Llywelyn also made peace with the dragons. He promised them protection within his realm, and his court magician, Defnyddwir Hud, wrought a spell to allow them to transform. In return, the ruling family of dragons—your family, Corsen—agreed to defend the realm. The agreement was made in this very building." He seemed inordinately proud of this, but I was too gobsmacked by what I heard to pop his smugness bubble.

"When the saesnich, backed by the dark power of the underworld, stole our freedom despite the best effort of your family, the descendants of Llewelyn the Last reaffirmed their promise. This university was founded as a place to preserve the knowledge that the saesnich would have destroyed. In the centuries since, one of your family has always been on campus, ready."

"Ready for what? And shouldn't I have known about this before…" I waved my arms around in emphasis.

"You should have. That is my mistake, Corsen. I believed, truly believed, the danger to Drake had passed. It's been over a century since the last attempt to gain the vaults." He took another bite of biscuit, looking remorseful.

I didn't speak, waiting for more information. After the biscuit was finished, he finally continued.

"I mentioned the saesnich had help from the underworld." I nodded. "That is a reason their damnable armies were rarely defeated in the Isles. Demonic creatures resembling men, but far stronger and more brutal. We call them orcs."

I coughed, spraying tea. "Orcs? Like Tolkien?"

Utterly unfazed by the tea now decorating his desk, Professor Gruffudd nodded. "Yes. He had special knowledge, being of the family Hud through his mother's side. We tried our best to obfuscate and add ambiguity, but even our efforts could not completely conceal the truth. Orcs exist and serve the Crown."

"I'm still trying to wrap my mind around this." I ticked points off on my fingers. "Orcs are real. I'm a dragon shifter, and my family defends Drake—hey, that makes sense now." He nodded. "So, what do I do now? Do I turn into a dragon? Won't that freak out the rest of the students?"

"No. We have time to get you to a safe place before your first transformation. After that, you'll be able to control when."

"There's a spot of good luck then." I still wasn't happy, and had way more questions than answers, but I was calmer. "How long do I have?"

"Let me see your arms."

I raised them up, noting the glow was now fully up to my shoulders. It didn't feel like anything, perhaps a bit of sunburn, but no worse than spending five minutes outside. He held them, running his hands over my jumper before letting them fall.

"Open your eyes wide, please."

This was odd, but I did. I always thought they were my best feature, a rich copper color I'd never seen outside my family.

"Hmm. Yes. Take off your cap." I was reluctant to lose the warmth the knit provided, but I was in this deep. What was a little more insanity? I removed it, and my red hair tumbled out of its confinement.

Unlike my eyes, I hated my hair. It was too bright, too in your face, and too much who I didn't want to be. No amount of bleach or dye would ever change it for more than a few days, and now, with these revelations, another penny dropped.

"I have red hair because I'm a dragon?" I was offended. What a cliché!

"It's the manifestation of your scales in human form, yes. Have you looked at it recently? Has the color changed?"

I grabbed a lock and pulled it in front of my eyes. Sure enough, instead of its usual muted orange, it was now a deeper, richer red, almost a vermillion.

"Yes."

"Hmm. I'd say you have an hour until you need to be under cover."

"Iacháu eich hynafiaid."

He chuckled. "That's not polite, Corsen."

Another thought popped into my head. "How are you involved? It can't be coincidental, you being my advisor."

He looked pleased at my conclusion. "No, no coincidence at all. The family of Llewelyn has always maintained their ties to yours."

"My parents didn't go to Drake."

"No, but several of your distant cousins have. There is always a McAdrich on campus, just as there always a Gruffudd."

I goggled. "You're a descendant—"

"Of Llewelyn. Yes." He gathered his hat and briefcase. "Come along. We have little enough time." He cast a glance at the door. "Must tell maintenance."

For an old man, he moved fast, and I had to hurry to keep pace. We passed through the corridors I knew, through a door to a steep stairwell which continued far beyond anything I expected. We were at least eight floors below ground when it finally ended in a rough-hewn stone archway.

"Professor?" He paused, but didn't turn. "Where are we going?"

"Drake was built over a system of caverns, which open on a cliff by the sea. It's the largest place we have available, since we don't know the size of your dragon."

How big was large?

I was going to find out. Soon, apparently.

The corridor beyond the archway turned into a natural cave within a few yards. It had been maintained, even modernized, with electric lamps and handrails that looked like they dated from the twenties. The 1920s.

It was at least a half-hour's walk to the cavern by the sea, and I took full advantage of the time. Every question I could think of about my heritage, the abilities of dragons, the tortuous history of my family and the university, I asked. Professor Gruffudd answered them all.

The glow continued to spread. I was glad it wasn't uncomfortable, or I would have been in a world of pain. I checked my hair, almost obsessively, and he was right. It was getting redder and redder with every minute.

At last, I could smell the sea and hear distant waves.

"Professor? I don't think I have much longer to wait. How big is this cav —"

We emerged from the channel onto a ledge, and my legs nearly gave out. It was enormous. A vast space rose above us, easily sixty feet, but down. Down was even more staggering. A hundred feet, easily, and wide as a football pitch. Giant spires rose from the floor, matched by others hanging from the ceiling, and I spent fruitless moments recalling which were stalactites and which were stalagmites before abandoning it.

"I believe you'll find the space adequate." Gruffudd's tone was Sahara dry.

"How big do you expect me to grow?" I whispered.

"Judging by the intensity of your hair and the color of your eyes, you may well be the largest dragon in three centuries. Perhaps longer."

He tugged me to my feet. "Not much further."

"What do you mean?"

Gruffudd pointed. There were stairs carved into the cavern wall. "We have to get to the bottom. You can't transform here; this ledge is certainly too small."

Stairs. No rail. And they looked slippery.

He looked back, already two steps down. "Come on, Corsen."

I balled up my courage and decided it was far too little for such a task. Instead, I focused my anger. If I could control it, maybe I could channel it to my feet, heat my trainers enough to dry the steps without melting the soles. It was worth a try.

Controlling the fflam, my inner dragon's power, was oddly easy. Natural in a way I'd never experienced before. Instinctive, almost. My feet warmed, and as long as I lingered on each step for a few seconds, my footing was secure.

I was surprised to see a smile on Gruffudd's face when I reached the bottom. Given the time press, I'd expected him to be angry, but he looked almost proud.

"Well done. Now, don't dawdle. We have only moments."

I stood, unsure of my next step.

He prompted me. "You need to disrobe, Corsen."

"What? No way!" Gruffudd was old enough to be my Bamps. I wasn't peeling out of my knickers in front of him.

"Unless you've brought a change of clothes, I highly recommend it. Walking through the campus back to your dorm starkers is probably a poor choice."

I hated it, but his logic made sense.

"I'll turn my back."

"Don't worry about it, Professor. If you're going to see me transform, you'll see me nude." I started peeling layers away, shivering almost immediately. "I h-hope it happens soon. It's bloody cold in here!"

He looked critically at my hair. "I'd say you could change as soon as you feel ready."

"Sometime next year th-then?" I was down to my undergarments.

"All you need to do is — "

"I know. Will it to happen and let my magic do the rest. You told me about seven times." I pulled off the bra, then my knickers. "Let's get this done."

He pointed. "Over there. The greatest clearance."

I groaned, but started trotting. "You c-couldn't tell me b-before I stripped?"

It was a wide clearing, free of any spires, and I stopped in the center.

"You may begin."

I closed my eyes. Though I didn't think I needed to, it couldn't hurt, right? I thought the words Gruffudd taught me.

Rhyddhau fy ddraig!

My expectations, my guesses, were totally wrong.

For starters, I thought it would hurt. It didn't. The magic pulsing through me was as if I was enjoying a warm bath from the inside. My veins filled with heat, and my body expanded to absorb it. When my wings sprouted from my back, it was no more than an itch. My neck, arms, and legs all lengthened, and I peered around to see my new wings. That's how I caught sight of the tail as it sprouted from my behind.

Fascinating.

My face stretched and deformed, my nose extending, my ears shifting to the top of my head, my eyes growing larger. My vision was sharper, too, and I could hear individual seagulls flying outside. I wriggled my tongue against the rows of sharp teeth I suddenly had.

The last changes were to my skin. It had gotten progressively pinker from my usual pallor, brought on by too many hours stuck inside; now, the scales Gruffudd promised appeared. I tapped one with a claw—claw? Yes, that was definitely a claw—and heard it clink. Armor.

When the last of the heat faded, I unfurled my wings and gave them a tentative flap.

It was glorious.

I felt the power in them, waiting to be unleashed.

Why would I want to be human? I was a bloody dragon!

"Corsen."

My attention was pulled down to Gruffudd. He looked insignificant. But then, he was only human.

"You must hurry. The orcs will attack at dark."

I knew, without looking, I had about forty minutes. How? Innate time sense? Magic? Who knew? I'd ask after.

"I'm going." My voice was mine, but not. The soft contralto was gone, replaced by a bass which was still undeniably feminine. I walked to the edge of the opening.

It was a long way down.

I shook off my nerves.

This was my moment.

I stretched my wings and jumped, letting instincts I didn't know were in me take over. My wings flapped, grabbed air, and my precipitous descent was turned into a climb into the rays of the sunset. My scales shimmered, and I knew my purpose.

I was a dragon, pledged to defend my university from orcs, not simply a woman with one degree in maths and another in astrophysics, staring at the stars, waiting for Christmas break to begin, and marking time until the next thing came along.

No.

That might be part of my life, but it wasn't *all* of my life. Not any longer.

I rolled, delighting in the feel of air rushing past me, and grinned.

Time to feast on some orcs.

ADAM GAFFEN

Adam Gaffen is an award-winning author best known for The Cassidy Chronicles, a near-future, hopepunk science fiction series centered on the adventures of Kendra and Aiyana Cassidy. His work spans multiple genres, including fantasy, romance, and science fiction, and he's been recognized with nominations for the DragonCon Dragon Awards and Page Turner Awards. Adam lives in Colorado with his wife, their five dogs, and five cats, enjoying a life full of writing and furry companions.

https://www.cassidychronicles.com

facebook.com/adam.gaffen
x.com/RabidChipmunk42
instagram.com/adamgaffen
threads.net/@adamgaffen

BLITZED

ILONA KRUEGER

T illy re-read the note in her pigeon hole, *'Application for leave over the Christmas period has been declined. Your presence is required to maintain operational levels. Two hours grace will be given to you as we shall open at 9 AM instead of 7 AM. Season's Greetings to you and your family. Justin.'*

Disappointment trickled through her. She had never had more than a day's leave over Christmas for several years. So much for the proud motto, 'Fair Go to All Employees.' Justin, the proprietor, knew about her challenges as a single parent having to juggle finances, mortgages, and childcare in the face of minimal permanent employment opportunities. She was not in a position to complain. Less-than-perfect job conditions were better than no job at all.

Often abrupt, dismissive, and pushy, Justin made her feel undervalued, stupid, and invisible, often blaming her for anything that went wrong. A well-meaning friend had suggested she report him, but it wasn't as easy as that. He was, after all, the boss, and she needed the job.

It was only a week to Christmas. He had okayed her application verbally six months ago and any time she had mentioned

31

her trip overseas, he'd said nothing to counter it. Could he really be so cruel? Did he have the right to do this?

Booked and paid for ages ago, the overseas flights were non-refundable. With only a few days before departure, everything was organized. Packing. Passports. Approval by her ex-husband for the children to leave the country. Her siblings lived in other parts of the world and were also going — not only for Christmas but also for their parents' surprise 50th wedding anniversary.

Wiping tears away from her eyes, Tilly resolved to see the day out. It was imperative she talk to Justin immediately, hopefully to appeal to his sense of fairness. She would even offer to do extra hours unpaid to make up for it. This was for her family. For her children who had never met their grand-parents. For her parents who were unable to travel.

Justin was nowhere on the premises. Other staff said he'd gone home early. Every time Tilly rang his number, the message droned out, 'Unavailable.'

Sad disappointment now honed into the sharp knife of anger. How could he do such an arrogant, unethical thing? Her base instincts wanted to smash everything in sight, just as he had smashed the joy of reunion with her family. Hate was not part of her usual nature, but right now, it surged in her, harnessing a lightning bolt of revenge.

"You look like you've just found a cockroach in your salad," her co-worker, Mark observed, simultaneously scrolling down messages on his phone.

"Worse than that! Much worse!"

"Wanna tell me about it?" Mark said, his back already turned to walk away.

"I don't know whether there are swear words strong enough to cover what I feel at the moment."

"Hey there, Silly-Tilly. Someone struck you in the Achilles? Never heard a swear word willy-nilly." Grinning widely at his poetic attempt, he continued scrolling through messages and memes on his phone. Serious conversation was impossible with Mark. She rued the moment she'd let it slip that her lifelong nickname was Silly-Tilly. Like a dog with a bone, he'd added it to his repertoire of clichés and meaningless blabber.

It seemed that her nickname was a legacy of personality. No one took her seriously. Always affable. Always willing to help. Always stepping away from conflict and re-guiding it to harmony. She wished she'd had the strength of character to overthrow those who belittled her. Her mind played games with her. "Shoot me," it said. "Lame duck that I am."

The question remained—how could Tilly resolve this eleventh-hour problem? Leave and be homeless? Or cancel the trip, lose money, and let everyone down? She was a failure. A loser. Everyone knew it, and so did she.

Tilly surveyed the Christmas tinsel scalloped around the wall of the dining area, lighting it up with Christmas cheer, the result of hours of her personal input beyond the call of duty.

But now, disdain smeared her face, and she fancied herself the best of the Bah Humbugs. What did it all mean anyway? Messages of peace and joy made her want to throw up. Who cared about Christmas anyway? She picked up the large, wooden Father Christmas near the register and envisaged it as firewood. The heat of her anger could have kindled it to flame.

She'd lock up later as was expected, but this time she would show him. She harnessed her anger, resentment, and frustration into something much bigger—revenge and action!

In a few minutes of intense rampage, Tilly stripped the place of every shred of Christmas paraphernalia, dumping it all in a heap on the floor of the preparation area. A quick scan of the restaurant area revealed a snow globe with an enchanting Christmas scene she hadn't noticed till now. Someone else must have brought it in.

Mesmerized, Tilly wound up the animation. Lights in shop fronts flicked on simultaneously with a chorus of familiar music. The quaint village and a frozen pond were backdropped by a forest of fir trees whose spicy aroma suddenly came into her presence. Sprinkled with silver stars, the midnight canopy glittered magically.

For a few moments, her anger subsided. The nostalgia of smiling memories and sparkling eyes, the joy that Christmas symbolized, cooled her feelings of hurt and disappointment.

Tilly sighed. She imagined herself as Starlight, the super-heroine who would instinctively know what to do. Nothing would faze her. Not like it did Wishy-Washy Silly-Tilly.

But this was just a pretend world. The snow globe encap-sulated dreams that could not be reached, fake realities that were harder to attain than the tallest of mountains. As the image of a smiling snake flashed before her, Tilly flung the snow globe to the tiled floor in disgust. She didn't care if it spewed glass in all directions, cracked the tiles, or even caused the boss injury. Such was the venom of her fury.

But...

It didn't break.

Puzzled, Tilly picked it up. It was intact and still in working order. The music kept playing *Have a holly, jolly Christmas*... A sardonic antithesis of her current mood.

"Shut up!" she screamed at it as she threw it again with an extraordinary force that only hate can muster. It still didn't break! As a last resort, she bashed it with a steel rolling pin, but the music still continued, the lights sparkled, and the little world danced to its own tune. The only thing shattered was her sense of hope. All that remained of the Season of Joy was a sad skeleton.

Exhausted, Tilly sat on the floor cradling the unbroken snow globe, her tears dripping onto the glass. She longed to be part of this idyllic world, where happiness was guarded and nothing could crack its composure. She closed her eyes and breathed deeply.

Moments later she was shivering. When she saw the snow around her, she was sure she had drifted into a dream, into the world of the snow globe, better by far than her world of broken hopes.

The cold penetrated her less-than-adequate work clothing. Snow began to fall in large, floaty flakes. She could actually see the intricate hexagon structure and its detail, usually imperceptible to ordinary sight. She cupped her hand to catch one and was immediately enveloped in warmth. A fur-like collar hugged her neckline and continued into a warm hood. Smoothing her hands over the fabric revealed the pleasure of satin, padded with warmth on the inside, wrapping her whole body with delectable softness.

The snowflakes skimmed over her face, pausing a moment on her fingertips, where her short, brittle nails had lengthened into phosphorescent ovals. Mirror-smooth, they enabled her to glimpse herself: her long brown hair, customarily imprisoned by hairpins and tie-backs, now cascaded from beyond her hood in caramel and golden silk. Her pale-blush lips intensified to an empowered fire-engine red. Determination became her most trusted friend.

Another snowflake kissed the tip of her nose. As it melted into her skin, the uncanny sensation that she was an incarnation of Starlight, heroine of her fictional ramblings, flitted into her consciousness.

Questions with no clear answers. How had she slipped into this portal world? Why was she here? How would she get home? Who could she trust? Why was there a sword at her feet? Was she expected to do battle? To kill or to defend? And what was meant by the words inscribed on the sword?

Matilda, embrace your name. Embrace your mission.

Matilda? How would anyone know?

From the distance, Tilly heard cries for help. Instinctively, she knew she was needed and ran toward the commotion. Smoky, pungent fires of burning wood irritated her lungs. She coughed and gasped. Christmas trees everywhere were aflame.

Sellers furiously tried to extinguish the flames with buckets of water and towels but were losing the battle as tree after tree caught a spark and succumbed to an ashen demise.

Without hesitation, Tilly held her sword out and whooshed it powerfully through the air—so powerfully that the flames were instantly quenched like candles on a birthday cake. But new fires kept erupting, extending toward the heavy forests beyond. Tilly wielded her sword vigorously for hours, quenching one after another, her face manifesting no sign of alarm, fear, or anger. Instead, she simply willed authority over the calamity. And when it was over, there was no hint of pride.

The villagers were more than impressed as they shouted acclaim, "Matilda, the Knight in White Satin, you have saved us from destruction."

The name was not new to her. Yes, she was Tilly, an affectionate diminutive of Matilda at home, but here she was a powerful responder, truly a Matilda, a strong woman. Her father had said to her a long time ago, "In times of trouble, Tilly, remember your birth name is Matilda. It designates innate strength of character. Use it wisely. Use it well." And her mother had added, "It's all a matter of timing, and you will embrace your real name."

She surveyed the charred scene, but thankfully the homes in the village were untouched by fire. Tilly...Matilda...stroked the backs of her hands as if brushing away dust, and as she did so, the phosphorescence on her nails drifted over to sad-looking tree remains. In moments, signs of rejuvenation appeared as they rose in triumph like a phoenix from the ashes.

The crowd hushed as they watched the remarkable scene unfold. And then they cheered in thankfulness and amazement.

Matilda held her sword high above her head, pointing to the stars.

"Stop!" she said, commanding silence. "Who did this?"

"There was a stranger who did it, M'lady. He lit all the fires."

"He was no one we've seen before. He looked like he came from another world. Not like us."

Indeed, the villagers wore clothes of a bygone era. On posts, lanterns filled with oil gave off soft light. There were a few horses and a carriage or two, presumably belonging to out-of-towners, but the locals went everywhere on foot, carrying their loads or using hand carts. Tales of hard physical labor lined their faces, yet the glow of the joy in the ordinary was evident.

"There he is now!" someone called out. In an instant, Matilda eagle-eyed him, and sensed familiarity. At first, she thought *Justin*, but she rationalized that her earlier preoccupation with him would likely have influenced her judgment. Nevertheless, his clothing and demeanor marked him as a stranger.

"Halt!" she commanded as he held his flaming torch to a modest village house. He ignored the order and proceeded to the next cottage.

"Halt!" she repeated. "There will be consequences." She strode over to him and slashed the torch out of his hand and onto the ground, stamping out the flames with her boots, trusting that no harm would befall her in doing so. Empowerment brought courage and trust. She whooshed her sword over the cottage fires before much damage was done and similarly scattered phosphorescence over the damage.

"Who are you? Speak now!" Matilda held her sword to his throat, so close that a sneeze from him would have killed him. Seemingly at her mercy, he used his own brand of defense. A dense, smoky cloud emanated, dragon-like, out of his nostrils obliterating her sight and unsettling her composure momentarily. It bought enough time for him to stand up and tower over her, swathed now in a flowing black cloak, dominating and intense as he proclaimed, "I am Hunter Jay and you will be quelled!" He twirled his handlebar mustache, obviously engrossed with delusions of grandeur. Despite his dramatic introduction, Matilda could not squash the notion of familiarity. And yet the menacing persona, Hunter Jay, did reciprocate recognition.

"Kill me now!" Matilda challenged. "If you have the stomach for blood."

"Ah, but I am Hunter Jay, and I am thrilled by the chase, not by a martyr's whining or sacrifice. In the meantime, I have work to do. I will not rest until Christmas is destroyed." And then, in a puff of smoke, he was gone, dissolved into the air. If only it were for good.

More cheering came from the villagers, sure the day had been won.

"See how our Lady Matilda disappeared him into that sooty air!"

"Trapped in his own game! Good riddance!"

"Hooray, we've won Christmas back!"

But Matilda was not so sure. Experience had taught her about bullies, masters of the cat-and-mouse game, the unrelenting destroyers of morale.

If they are permitted to do so.

Nevertheless, the celebratory atmosphere was welcome. It was short-lived, however, when a tinkling bell preceded the arrival of a woebegone-faced reindeer that collapsed in their midst, moaning with pain and heartbreak.

"Someone get water, food, and a blanket," Matilda ordered. "Check for injuries." She snatched the note attached to the bell collar:

'Guess who? Out of sight, out of mind? Wrong! Santa Claus is coming to town! As DINNER! Yum! The oven is ready as we speak. And watch out reindeer!'

Alarm seized Matilda. Tremors of horror ricocheted across the village. Consequences would be abysmal here and in her world. Children would be traumatized. Tradition would be cast into obscurity. Songs would be forgotten. Anticipation would be kicked in the backside. Trimmings and decorations would sit in a shed to rot or become landfill. No more December countdown.

Quick action was imperative. Where to start?

"Where will I find an oven big enough to fit Santa in?" she called out.

"You're not going to incinerate him, are you?" a few of the villagers demanded.

Realizing the ambiguity of her words, Matilda countered, "NO! But Hunter Jay intends to!"

"The Brickwork Kiln outside the village! That's where!"

"Take me there!" All was haste, no time to waste. She followed the leaders, her sword beaming out a path of light, closely tailed by the well-recovered reindeer and the rest of the village. Time was on their side. Moments later they were there. But where was Santa?

A cacophony of rattling bells caught their attention. There, high on the chimney stack was Santa yelling for help while his reindeer helpers honked hysterically, also clinging on in fear. Below, Hunter J, with pitchfork and butcher knife, was ready for the kill as they slowly slid to their fate. The kiln had already been fired up, and the aroma of onions and garlic warmed by transferred heat from the kiln meant that dinner was on the way.

"I see you have come for the feast," Hunter J sneered. "Mistake though, because you're next." He clanked his knife and fork jubilantly. "And here comes the first volunteer. Which one are you? Donner or Blitzen? Never mind, I'll blitz you in no time. And you…" He directed his stare at Matilda. "Come closer, and you'll be first."

And then there'd be no way to help the others. The frightened, crying animal was precariously close to knifepoint. Matilda directed a light beam from her sword to the deer. Instinctively, it knew it was the rope to safety. In quick succession, although initially ambivalent, the others followed.

Santa was more hesitant. Aside from his bulky size, he had

a sack of presents slung over his shoulders. It was a wonder he was still hanging on. As he touched the light beam with his boot, it transformed into a strobing line of light.

Hunter J, astounded initially by the unusual rescue method, now sneered maliciously, his face lighting up with pleasure. Santa was his primary target, and he aimed to intercept the rescue of Santa. He lunged toward Matilda to disarm her of her sword with his knife, unaware that a few of the villagers had simultaneously formed a human chain to thwart him, causing him to trip, his knife flying from his grip. Before he could get up, they pinned him down by sitting on him, his demands for them to desist going unheeded. One of them reached for the butcher's knife.

"Bring it here!" Matilda commanded. "Touch the tip into the beam. But only the tip, no more. Do *not* touch the sword."

Amazingly, the dotted line of the sword-beam solidified, and Santa was brought down to safety, amidst cheering from all the villagers, including those who had Hunter J pinned down. Taking advantage of their lapse in focus, he muscled his way to freedom, snatched his knife back, and held it menacingly close to Matilda's neck.

"Kill me!" Matilda dared. "Or perhaps a duel might interest you."

"You'll see Santa dead first. No more Christmases for you, for anyone!" He clashed his knife against Matilda's sword as if he were clinking glasses.

Mistake!

The knife became butter, useless as a feather for fighting. He threw it away in disgust and reached for the sword instead, but when his hand contacted the sword, it became as ineffectual as a stick of putty. Within moments, his body disintegrated like a melted snowman, nothing remaining but his curling black mustache.

Happiness reigned.

The reindeer had retrieved the missing sleigh and other

scattered sacks of presents. Christmas would go ahead. Santa thanked everyone and promised them a bonus this year. The villagers suggested a celebration with hot, mulled wine for the adults and spiced hot chocolate for the children.

But Matilda wanted to go home to her own time, to her children.

But how? She looked at her sword for clues. Glowing letters popped out.

B-U-R-N-I-T

Burn what? An image of a mustache flashed before her briefly, and she knew. In an instant, Tilly snapped it up and threw it into the kiln. A blink later she was back in the preparation area next to the pile of destroyed decorations, the snow globe in her hands.

Had she imagined all this? She sighed. Time to go home.

Heading toward the car, she almost jumped out of her skin when something touched her shoulder.

"Tilly…" It was Justin, returning from his day away from the restaurant.

"My name is Matilda. Don't ever forget that!"

"Noted." He handed her an envelope.

"Don't bother. I've made my mind up. I'm not canceling my trip. You know what you can do with this." She handed him the denial of leave note. "I'm catching my plane as scheduled whether you like it or not."

Confused, Justin read the note and laughed, stirring Tilly's hostility even more.

"Fortunately for you, I am classy enough to refrain from swearing at you, but where fairness goes, you are severely lacking. Why don't you try living up to your name, Justin? Apply some justness and you'll get along fine with everyone." She was about to rip up the envelope, but Justin stopped her.

"Open it."

Inside was a transfer slip to her bank account for $2,000 with a note attached. *Thank you for all your efforts in keeping this place running so well. I couldn't do it without you. Sorry for my abrupt-ness at times. Enjoy your trip. Justin Hunter.'*

"What about this?" Tilly pointed to the refusal note, puzzled.

"Wrong pigeon hole—a late request from one of the casual staff. I felt off-color this morning and left a note for you. Probably got mixed up."

"Ohh," said Tilly. "How are you now?"

"I slept it off. Fine now." Justin replied. "Although I had this weird dream… There was this strange place where they tried to sabotage Christmas and kill Santa. Now who would do that?"

Tilly's throat was dry. "I don't know… Thank you for the bonus."

"No, thank *you*…Matilda." He smiled. "Anyway, I'm going back in to check a few things. Knowing you, everything will be in order. I love all the decorations."

Whoops…

ILONA KRUEGER

Ilona Krueger lives in the Nepean Valley, in Sydney, known for its stifling summer heat. She writes poetry and fiction, largely for herself but variously published. Several novels are in process, contending with her other assorted interests of gardening, imagining, needlecrafts, dreaming, pen pals, and creating. Her dollhouse is awaiting furnishing. Her toy room brings back childhood delight. Although German is her native language, she taught English, History and Languages for many years. Now it's time for coffee.

 instagram.com/ilonakrueger
 amazon.com/author/ilonakrueger

TAROT OF LOVE

CASSIE SWINDON

Winter air bites my cheeks, so I pull my red scarf tighter around my neck. I swear the cold feels more wicked after the sun sets. Maybe even more so when standing at the base of an ancient structure designed for nightmares and ghost stories. The shadows curling around the corners of the building are a piece of art only a storyteller could describe.

I've never done a tarot reading in a haunted castle before, but when Dane Brier DMs you with advanced payment, followed by a black heart emoji, a girl's only option is to agree wholeheartedly. I assumed the last time I'd ever see his devious face was seven months ago when we threw our graduation caps into the air. We walked across the stage, then went our separate ways with bachelor's degrees in hand.

It's ironic that my academic pursuits landed me here, a job no parent would want for their child. Not that I'm a kid anymore. Twenty-one is old enough to create enough damage with just the right pinch of naivety to still hope for a bright future. My magical powers enhance the tarot card readings to give the customer a full-fledged experience unlike any other. A strong gut feeling tells me that tonight's reading will be one of legends.

Dane's urgent message came out of the blue. Speaking of blue, my lips are probably a shade of death by now. Where is he? In two minutes, I'm speeding out of here faster than you can say, "Christmas disaster."

If I'm not home in time, I'll ruin Pop's two-decade-long streak of trying to scare me when the clock strikes midnight. What can I say—some traditions are worth the hassle. So, if Dane knows what's good for him, he better appear around that pine tree in the next...

An engine rumbles in the distance, short spurts of an accelerator followed by an easy buzz. He still rides a motorcycle despite how many times I showed him pictures of smashed brains on the side of the road. Fan-freakin'-tastic. One more thing I need to worry about.

He whizzes closer, tires shooting a blast of snow behind the bike. Well, if any Deadern creature plans to attack, Dane sure left an easy trail to follow. Since his helmet is still on, I can't see his face yet. It's only been seven months, but does he still wear the same black eyeliner? Has he cut his hair to fit an office job, or is it still wild and shaggy? It might be the end of the world if Dane surrendered to a corporate career already. At least his fashion seems consistent: tight jeans, which I've always admired. The red plaid jacket is new, though. Heat climbs up my cheeks when I realize my skirt matches his jacket. Of course I'd be unconsciously connected to this man, even after our time apart.

"Sofie?" He parks his bike and swings one leg over the side. "Is that you?"

I clear my throat and adjust my stilettos in the snow. Yes, my outfit is the worst possible choice for this meeting, but he messaged me while I was at Zo's party. It's not like the guy granted me extra time to run home and change.

I nod. Or maybe I just stand there like an ice sculpture

because my brain has stopped working. Time slows down when he slips his helmet off and flashes me the damned smile that has ruined my life. And yes, his eyeliner has remained, thank Goddess Above.

"You're blonde now!" Dane steps forward with both arms wide open for a hug.

I'm confident he's never hugged me before. Instantly, I take a step back and study him. He stops in place, brows rising in confusion. My eyes dip low, then follow his tire tracks to give me something else to focus on other than his gorgeous, dark eyes.

"Oh, right. My bad." With a sweep of his hand and a spark of light that flies from his fingertips, the trail his bike left vanishes.

My heartbeat pounds on overdrive, threatening to break my ribs in half. When was the last time I took a breath? In. Out. Good. Breathe, Sofie. He's one person. One silly, insanely intelligent, creative person who I've cast a thousand spells with. Grow up and act like an adult.

"Yup, blonde today. Maybe pink tomorrow," I say casually.

"Am I allowed to hug you?" He throws those long arms open again.

"Uh, okay, but I'm in a bit of a rush."

Dane's smile turns upside down. "Oh, gotcha. Well, let's get started, then."

I lead the way, careful where I step, yet hear his audible inhale when I sink low and snow coats my shins.

"Um, do you want me to...?"

"No, I got it." With a flick of my wrist, I hover above the snow and glide onto the front steps of the castle. Or maybe it's a chateau. I've never known the difference.

He follows silently, but I know he's near from the overflowing energy exploding from his aura. Something's different. The grief he carried has been plucked from his spirit like a grape from a vine. Maybe it was the space away from me that helped him heal. That'd be quite a downer to consider.

"So, do we knock?" He bites his lip and studies the old door.

I can feel his stare on my cheek, but don't dare turn. The second we make eye contact will be my doom.

"Nah, we've never been one to follow rules before. Why start now?"

"Touché." He nods. "May I have the honors, Sof?"

I gesture for him to enter first, which he does without hesitation, as fearless as his wolf familiar used to be… Before her death. My chest clenches at the memory. Now isn't the time to consider 'what ifs.'

Inside, sinister chandeliers drip from the ceiling. I'm instantly obsessed. Every ounce of my soul knows I'd live here till my dying day if given the chance. Little jitters form deep in my belly and travel across my whole body—the best type of omen.

Above, a few specters float, as expected, but we're not here to visit them. Unable to stop myself, I scan the giant staircase that rises to the second floor like a setting in a fairytale novel.

"The silence is deafening," Dane whispers, so close to my ear that another shudder tingles my neck. "I've got an idea," he says, then cups his mouth with his hands and starts to sing the lyrics to the song we wrote together once upon a time: *"Loooooonesome dragon burn them down. I trust you from here below…* Come on, Sof. Sing with me."

"Nah, I'll start shuffling the cards."

He takes the deck, sets it on the ground, and kisses the top of my hand. "I will not give up until you sing with me."

Warmth floods through my skin. What evil is he trying to destroy me with? This isn't fair.

I sigh and join in.

"Loooooonesome dragon burn them down
I trust you from here below

All the spirits in our town
Echo words from years ago."

Dane lifts me fast and spins me in a circle. "Goddess, I've missed you, Sof."

I swallow the emotions rising up my throat, ignore the fluttering in my stomach, and command my heart rate to slow the ef down. Once he places me back on the ground, I savor a single moment in his solid arms, the place I've always desired to settle.

Avoiding his eyes, I shrink into a sitting position in the middle of the massive room. "I heard a blizzard might hit tonight, so let's focus."

He follows suit, aware of my methods. I spread the cards out, face down so he can't see the image they portray. I suck in a deep breath and collect my courage, then finally meet his eyes.

Warm browns stare back, full of mischievous memories and unmade promises. I've needed this time away from Dane to see clearly—that we are never meant to be, that he is looking for something else, or maybe someone else? Our past together may have been the best friendship of my life, but I'm certain I made the right choice in moving away.

Right?

"Peek-a-boo. I see you." His smile debilitates me.

Why? Why me?

I shake my head, then force myself to keep looking into his eyes. "Think of the question you'd like guidance on."

"Got it already," Dane says, tapping his temple softly. "Been holding on to it for a while."

I motion for him to stop talking. "I don't want more info."

It looks like he's holding back a chuckle, but he nods respectfully.

"Touch three cards that call out to you."

"Easy peasy." He taps three in a row without contemplating first, not his usual style.

A bone chilling shriek fills the air, cascading down the stairs from the second floor. We exchange a knowing glance, and his face turns as serious as my Pops when he slices the prize ham for Christmas Eve dinner, which will be starting any minute now. The first holiday supper I'm not present for, ever since I was born. Because I'm sitting on the floor with a man I'm in love with, willing to do anything to make him happy. What if this is my last moment with Dane? What if we part ways once more and this is the real goodbye? I must make the most of it.

"Your first card," I say, while flipping it over, "is the Devil of Hearts."

I can't breathe. It's too perfect. Of all the times I've ever practiced reading for him, he's never chosen this card. Dumbfounded, I stare at him, and unwilling to hold back, I ask, "What changed since May?"

His smile returns, but his eyes keep glancing to the stairway behind me. "All in good time, my dear. Be patient… Do you want to interpret now or after all three?"

"Now. Hold my hand."

He does, as always, without a beat of hesitation, like I'm his lifeline, his anchor, his tie to what's both real and magical in the same breath. But it's only a wish. I snap my fingers, and we're transported to another location, the scene morphed.

This part of the reading is as surprising to me as it is for any customer. In our new setting, it's still winter, and we're still under the moon, but we've moved to the center of a circle of pinecones. In this dream-world, I could hypothetically look like anything to Dane. But I'm not who matters in this situation.

Dane glows with obvious love in his heart, so consumed by his feelings for someone that the pinecones meld together to form a unified fortress, protecting him from any danger lurking outside the circle.

With the knowledge that everyone responds differently to

this stage, I gently whisper the interpretation. "This is good, Dane. Whoever you care for returns your feelings, just as strong. You're safe with them and you don't need to worry about being yourself."

Before I can grasp more details, we're whipped out of the scene and brought back to the floor of the castle. There's no telling how long we were gone for, seconds or hours. Too bad for Pops and his trophy ham. My head feels a little dizzy and the first bout of fatigue has set into my bones. Peculiar. Usually I don't feel so tired so quickly.

That's when I realize Dane's still holding my hands. Also strange.

"I'm ready," he nods to the second card.

I let go of one of his hands to flip the second. Again, I'm utterly and entirely shocked. My palms turn clammy at the possibility of the meaning of this next image.

"Go on, Sof. Tell me."

"It's the…the Grave of Wolves."

"That's right. Let's go take a trip." He scoots closer, and his gaze drops to my lips, as if…almost as if he's going to…

We spin away from the castle and land in a flowery clover field where a mound of dirt is higher than the rest of the tall grass. I look over, expecting to see Dane on his knees, forehead on the ground, tears falling from his face in grief. Instead, he's playing in the field with a gray pup whose eyes sparkle with cunningness. I hold back my own tears. He linked with a new familiar. The part of Dane that had been missing is restored. Even if we finish his reading now, I'd call this a success.

Wait. But Dane already knows this. He doesn't need a tarot card read, me, or someone else to inform him of his new bond. So, why did that card call out to him?

We're whisked away and become rooted back in the sitting position in the middle of the castle. Wind thunders against the high window panes. Must be the start of the incoming storm. How long have we been here?

I have a strange sensation of being watched and glance over my shoulder. Behind a grand piano, an adolescent wolf sits, wagging her tail.

"Come here, Chloe." Dane taps the ground, and she leaps toward him, ears happier than a kid on a snow day.

Don't tell that to my little brother, though. He'd never believe you.

I pet Chloe's soft fur and let her nuzzle into my neck and sniff my outfit. Hot tears betray me. She's perfect. Different than Mona, but exactly what Dane needs. If only I could also fit into that category. He's the only man who has seen the depths of who I am without hiding or running in fear. I need that acceptance more than I need air. Last May I was stupid enough to run first, before I was left behind.

"And the third card?"

Another eerie howl charges from upstairs. A harsh warning much stronger than before. We don't have much time left.

I bite my lip, memorize the moment. This is it. There's no coming back from this card. After the third setting is finished, we'll separate. I'll magically arrive back home at my parents' front stoop. And Dane, with Chloe, will be transported to the place of his choosing.

I need more time. It feels like my chest is about to explode with unsaid words. Like my body is too small for the feelings tossing around like wild waves in the sea. I can't let him go without saying how I feel once. Just once. Right after I flip the card, I'll say it.

I turn over his last card and gasp at the sight of my card. "The Queen of Magic."

Dane's smile has never been wider, brighter, or more authentic. "It was always you. I just hadn't known before."

"Dane. I…"

Loud, tromping hooves stampede upstairs. They're here. We both rise to our feet, hands out, ready to fight. Light already sparks from Dane's fingertips as he creates an orb of protection.

"Take my hand, and we'll leave."

"Shit, no." He licks his lips. "Finish what you were going to say, first."

Ten creatures… No, at least two dozen Deaderns storm down the stairs at full speed, antlers pointed straight at the barrier. If they're magically enhanced, they'll slash straight through without breaking a sweat.

"Dane! There's no time to talk!"

"There's always time for a proclamation of love, Sof!"

He flicks his wrist and gold glitter forms the shape of a deadly spear. It surges forward. Guts the lead Deadern in the chest. He collapses to the ground in a heap. Which trips one of the others.

"Hurry!" I reach out, but Dane's too far away.

"Look at me!" He yells, "I love you, Sofie! I couldn't stand the pain of losing Mona last year, and I turned into the worst type of person. I'm sorry I was so terrible. But you never gave up on me."

Sharp antlers shred through the barrier. Their crazed, bloodthirsty snarls compete with Chloe's growls.

"Take my hand!" I leap toward Dane, knowing he'll catch me.

Right before the Deaderns snap us in half, Chloe jumps to Dane as well. The three of us swirl in a confusing, snowy vortex. My feet are over my head. I'm tangled in a mass of pretzeled limbs and tight grips. Fur presses against me. Then a hand grabs my waist so possessively, I don't have to open my eyes to know he's here—Dane's safe. We escaped. In the background, the shrieks and shrills fade away until we topple onto a cobblestone street in a heap of heavy breaths and quiet *are you okays*.

Under the moon, little houses line the street, waiting for the next morning when each child will open their gifts. This can't be right. We're in my parents' neighborhood. The familiar bell tower strikes from the town square behind me. I count to eleven, then let my shoulders finally relax. Before I know it, Dane's laughing. He pulls me in close for that hug I had avoided. Then his earlier words finally hit me. He loves me?

"When?" I lean toward Dane, sharing the same air. "How?"

"Always." Snowflakes land on his nose. "Because you're mine. And I'm yours."

His lips part in welcome. But he doesn't close the distance. After everything we put each other through, after he confessed his feelings, it's up to me to seal the deal.

Do I want him? More than anything.

Am I terrified of the future? Definitely.

Is fear worth the risk? Only the tarot cards know all the answers.

Trembling, I wrap my arms around his neck. His skin is so warm, so alive. This man, who's full of such passion, may unravel me to my very core. Maybe that's how love is supposed to be, a bearing of one's essence, of what lies in the center of the layers built in protection.

I press my lips to his, soft at first, tentative and exploring. Time stands still. He tastes like apple pie and cinnamon, like a bottled spell or a secret poem. I pull him closer, harder, unwilling to ever let go. He's right. I'm his. And he's mine. Forever. Nothing can stand between us.

Once I hit the point where I'll suffocate if I don't sneak in a breath, I break apart from him. I press my forehead to his.

"I love you too, Dane. Always have. Always will."

CASSIE SWINDON

When I got married in 2011, my husband and I flipped a coin to decide if we'd move to Portland, OR, or Raleigh, NC. They were the cities we visited in college and loved the vibes of both.

Like most things in life, I won, and we have lived in Raleigh ever since. Our daughter followed soon after, and then SURPRISE... When she was eight months old, we learned that her little brother was on the way. Now, with six fur babies, we have a full house of paws and little toes.

I started writing in 2020 during the "Renaissance" that was Covid. One morning, I awoke from a dream about two characters and wanted to write their story. That first trilogy didn't fully encompass my genre since I love the escapism of fantasy, so I switched to writing fantasy romance in a modern-day setting.

Interesting tidbits: I injure myself on almost every vacation; I've been to four big-name concerts front row and own a pair of Michael Phelps's personal goggles.

CassieSwindon.com

facebook.com/CassieSwindon

x.com/CassieSwindon

instagram.com/cassie_swindon_author

bookbub.com/profile/cassie-swindon

amazon.com/stores/Cassie-Swindon/author/B091N72414

THE PERFECT CHRISTMAS

J. T. MORIARTY

Christmas is a special time when magic is in the air, even in places where it never snows. Anticipation tickles everyone's nose and sweet treats are eaten faster than they can be set out. Jolly green, cheeky red, and pristine white decorate everything, getting everyone excited. Except for one little individual... Robot.

His heart and head were made of metal, but that didn't make him cold inside. Rather, with a smart, dinky, steel body, shiny arms and legs, and a red cap of metal, he stood proudly at only seven inches high. This little robot wasn't excited — they were daydreaming.

"I know what Christmas is all about," Robot announced to all his friends. "Christmas is about cheer and happiness, but more than that, it's about *hope*. I hope there are young kids — the good ones — opening presents on Christmas morning! Their eyes will light up, and it'll be exactly the present they want. Then they'll be happy, and the day will continue that way, right up until they've had too much dessert before bed. What do you think?"

The robot turned to his friends — a large collection of toys he had gathered together. At the front sat a teddy bear wearing a blue bow. To the side sat a green train and a princess dolly with two blonde pigtails. All three toys stayed perfectly still and didn't respond.

"Exactly my point!" Robot chirped in response. "Now, I picture the sweetest little girl. She has blonde hair— so much like your princess—not brown, because everyone's got brown hair these days. And do you know—" Robot paused, looking around, then mumbled, "What was that?"

The robot interrupted itself, pretending that the bear had said something.

"Well, how should I know if the child has dyed their hair or not? I can only go off appearances. Now…" Robot raised its arms in contemplation. "As I was saying, she has blonde hair in two ponytails, and she wears blue because that's her favorite color, and she's got jean overalls on, but the knees are ripped up."

Robot stopped, looking at the toys for a response. The drum set, placed precariously over the farmhouse, finally lost its grip and toppled sideways, going *ba-ðoom-tish!*

"I'm not joking," the robot snapped sternly. "That's the perfect Christmas, don't you know? Well, I should say *my* perfect Christmas, because everyone else's is different. But that sums up Christmas to me."

This was where it lived, in a nice big room full of nuts and bolts and other robot items. On a wooden table sat a pair of doll heads, some spare eyes of green and brown, leg extenders, and a set of crooked replacement antennae. On a shelf rested an oiling can, just in case of emergency. It had seen The Wizard of Oz, after all. Under the shelf was a wobbly bench with stained rags strewn about. In the other corner stood a mirror that Robot used to look at itself as it repaired little holes with molten slag. The bucket of slag had cooled solid long ago, but it would reheat it when the time came.

Robot stared longingly at a window that looked out of the repair room. Since no one was around, it pushed a small chair against the wall, then a larger one. Grunting and puffing in a metallic wheeze, Robot worked as excitement fluttered through its little chest. Finally satisfied with his makeshift chairs, it quickly scuttled up the legs and seats and to the top to peer out the window. Starlight drifted in, gleaming on its silver body as it took in the sight outside. White and merry, like soft silk had been placed over the world, while the sky itself was a swirling, black blanket. Twinkle lights covered all houses on the street, making the place magical.

"I do wish it was Christmas all year long. Don't you, chair?" Robot patted its newest friend affectionately. The chair, much like the toys, didn't respond. "Of course you do!" Robot answered for it.

Seeing all the houses made the robot think of the children living inside. All of their smiling faces—and even the kids with no teeth! Some with messy bed hair, and others who brushed it out, and all of them, no doubt, wearing their pajamas. Then, a worrying thought crept into Robot's head. How did it *know* the kids would have a great Christmas morning? Hope was one thing, but to be certain? To actually see it? That was the real proof!

"Oh dear, oh dear," the robot said to itself. "We'll have to come up with some way to be certain! We can't leave it to chance, oh no!" It rapped gently on the chair with its foot. "Chair, lower me to the ground. I have a plan to hatch."

It waited, giving the chair time to comply, but after a moment, the Robot let itself down and gave the chair a reassuring pat. "You're a very busy chair, I understand."

The little robot marched with determination down the hallway, found the room with the pencils and crayons and scratch paper, and set to work.

Sometime later, and with many broken pencils and holes in the sheet of paper, Robot had drawn its plan. "Perfect. This will work. You there, teddy bear!" Robot pointed at a fuzzy brown bear at the far end of the room and held up the wildly

59

scribbled ideas. "Look at this. That's me, hidden behind the beautifully-wrapped present. The one with green and white diagonal stripes. See here? And then, I've cut some *holes* in it so I can see outside. I'll be hidden in plain sight! And then I'll get to watch some children opening their toys, and that's how I'll make sure everything goes perfectly for Christmas. Okay?"

The teddy bear, who so far hadn't paid any attention, continued to look at the plan in serious contemplation before it also failed to respond.

"Geez, tough crowd," Robot said. Still, with hope in its metal heart, it spun on its heel and set about putting the plan into action.

Christmas was in two days, and Robot had to work quickly. Sneaking into the office supply store, it found a large sheet of white cardboard and green markers from the desk.

Robot drew a series of squares on the cardboard and carefully cut them out with scissors. There wasn't much time left before Christmas to have to fire up the slag for a quick self-repair! After ten minutes of snipping, Robot began assembling the squares by folding them into a 3D box.

At this point, the robot kicked the carpet and swore in robot language. "Nuts and bolts! I've forgotten the glue!" It would take some time to climb back up the chair leg, but the robot had to do it. While it did so, it thought of all the other items it would need to complete the box. String, no doubt, and a red bow. So many things!

An idea occurred to the robot just as it reached the top of the desk.

"I know! I'll just take everything I need *right now*. Then I won't ever have to come up here again!" The robot turned and patted the chair again, saying, "Thanks for being with me while I thought things through. You really helped."

The chair, of course, didn't respond.

Suddenly, Robot threw everything off the desk. A roll of red ribbon fluttered toward the floor. A purple marker dropped, followed by all the other colors. A cardboard tube (just in case), an entire pencil case, a little figurine of a Goblin wearing a dirty dress and holding a black flower, some staples, a computer mouse, and finally, the big potted plant.

"Wait a minute," said Robot, picking up the potted plant and holding it uncertainty over its head. "I don't need *this*." Robot put the potted plant down carefully before returning to its fevered job of knocking everything *else* off the table. "I need more room!"

All the noise, however, had alerted something else. Tall, large, and human. Whoever it was started to come closer, clearly wanting to investigate.

Robot was so busy, it didn't hear the footsteps approaching the room or grow scared when the lights were flicked on, and it failed to notice the shadow of the giant's hand until it was too late.

The hand grabbed the robot and lifted it off the ground. "Oh no!" Robot screamed and kicked. "Who are you? Let me go!"

"*Beep boop! Ba-∂a-boo!*" was all the human heard as they stuffed the funny little robot into a bag and walked out of the room.

It was dark and cold wherever Robot was. It had dried glue on the left side of its head and some cardboard stuck on its backside, but otherwise, it seemed unharmed. Just trapped. "Hello?" Robot called out. "Is anyone out there?" It groped at the darkness. The prison felt like the inside of a cloth bag. "I've been caught by some mistake. Hello? I'm not meant to be in here. I'm making a spy box so I can watch kids open their toys on Christmas morning! Hello?"

Robot gulped in surprise at its own words. "Was I planning

to *spy* on kids? What a rotten thing to do! But how else am I going to make sure Christmas goes perfectly?"

A little upset, Robot sat down in its cloth prison, holding its little head in its hands. It cried tiny, robot tears (which weren't really tears at all), and after a few moments, it went sadly to sleep.

The next thing Robot knew, it was startled out of sleep by a huge thump to the right, and then another to the left. It couldn't see anything but stood up all the same, trying to back away from the sound. "What's happening?" Robot yelled, hoping someone would hear. "Did I sleep through the night? It's Christmas tomorrow!"

Almost in response, it felt the cloth bag suddenly lifting up. Someone was carrying the bag again. "Hello? I say, hello! Let me out. I need to get back to the arts and crafts room! Please! I don't want to make the spy-box present anymore. I know that was the wrong idea. I need to think of something else! Are you listening to me?"

All the human could hear coming from inside the bag was *beep, ba ∂um tzzk!*

"Silly thing! It must be broken," said the human, walking down the hallway and into the garage. They pressed a button and the automatic garage doors began to open.

When the human spoke, all Robot understood was "Sii gaar daa?" The human spoke in a very slow, very thick voice, which Robot couldn't understand. While Robot was puzzling over the human's words, it heard a noise it recognized—the garage door! That was where the metal trash can was kept. That was where the humans threw out broken plates, old things, and even garbage!

"I'm not garbage!" yelled Robot, even louder now. "I swear, I'm good! I'm working! I'm quite smart! I made that fake present from nothing. I figured it all out myself! Hello! Are you listening to me?" For a moment, Robot paused and thought about the fact that no one had been listening to it lately. Maybe no one could understand? "Stop! Let me out!" Robot had to keep trying.

Despite all the little robot's protesting, the bag never opened. The robot felt itself being carried across the room. It heard the sound of metal on metal as a lid was pulled off what sounded like…a giant trash can…

While waiting in the dark for what felt like a day and a night, Robot thought about exploring its new surroundings. Was it Christmas now? Had it missed Christmas morning? Where was it now? Where did the trash *go*? What *had* the human said?

Still stuck within the bag, Robot tried reaching out and found something solid like a wall beyond the fabric. It couldn't tell if it was feeling the metal sides of the trash can or something else. "I do think there's been a mistake here, human," Robot said bravely, finding its little voice in the dark. "You're going to be so embarrassed when you find out!" Robot tried a giggle but sounded more like a mouse.

Silence was the only response. To distract itself, Robot began thinking about the hideaway present. "If only I had brought the scissors," it thought. "Then I could cut myself free!"

Eventually, what little light there was disappeared entirely. The sounds of household action were very distant, but the scrape of cutlery and plates was heard, then some water running, and finally, feet going upstairs.

After what seemed like forever, the sound of feet returned. The darkness was became one shade lighter when a switch turned on. It wasn't much, all Robot could see now was its little, clawed hands, but at least that was something.

"Hello, human? I'm stuck in this bag. Help me!"

There was a great motion as the bag shifted upward, and Robot fell on its head. A sudden, glaring light poured into the bag from above, and Robot shielded its eyes. A giant hand—the same one—came down into the bag and grabbed Robot by the feet.

"Unhand me! I have things to do!" Robot protested, but it was useless. Almost as though the human couldn't hear it, they continued handling the little robot, ignoring its protests.

Robot was carried across the room, where it was thrown into a box of some sort. The box was closed entirely, and then the sound of ripping and scratching came from outside the box. "Oh no, I'm being sealed away!" Robot cried. "This is worse than the trash can! Maybe I could have made my way here or found another home—one where the humans like a good, smart robot such as myself. Now, I'm trapped."

Desperate, Robot banged against the walls of this new prison, but its feeble little fists did nothing, made no sound, and the movement was certainly not enough to alert a human. "I'm doomed," Robot cried some more. "I'll be in here until my battery pack runs out. Then I'll just melt away into battery acid and reflux. What a way to go."

The next morning came suddenly with a series of bumps and thumps on Robot's head. "Hey, what's this now?" Someone was jostling the prison Robot was in, kicking and pushing it around, no doubt. "This really will not do!"

Muffled voices outside the prison walls were warped and slow to Robot's ears, and it strained to understand anything.

Suddenly, almost as bright as before, there was a slice of light before a great, burning illumination washed down into the box, and Robot was blinded again. "No, no! I've had enough!"

A hand reached down into the prison, grasping Robot, but it was a much smaller hand this time. Softer, too. "What is this?" asked a curious little voice, high and joyful.

Robot blinked in amazement. It was a human voice, but this one it could understand. "Huh-hello?" Robot tried. It tried looking at who the hand belonged to, but its eyes were still adjusting from the sudden light.

"Oh my gosh, it's a robot!" came the bird-sweet voice again. "Just like the one I wanted!"

Robot was squeezed against the child's chest, and when it was pulled back it took a look at its new owner. A pretty little girl with freckles dotting her nose and blonde hair done in two pigtails. Her gorgeous eyes, like chocolate buttons, gazed adoringly at Robot.

"Well, hello there," Robot said simply, not knowing what else to say.

Two more humans were lounging on couches before a huge, green tree that smelled of pine. Beneath the tree, in various colors and prints and decked with tinsel and bows, sat about fifty presents. Some were already open with wrapping paper strewn all over the floor.

"Was it Christmas *today*?"

"Yes, it's Christmas!" giggled the little girl, hugging the little robot against her face.

"And you can understand me?"

"Of course I can, silly."

This was too great. Robot was overcome with sheer joy. "Then Merry Christmas!" Robot said, hugging the girl back.

The mother and father smiled contentedly, watching their daughter fuss over the little robot. "What do you think it's saying?" The mother asked the father.

"I haven't the faintest idea," said the father, "but it was beeping all night long. I just fiddled with its wiring a bit, and now, it's good as new."

At lunchtime, the family sat at the dining room table covered in food. The father placed chicken on everyone's plate while the mother served the vegetables. Jenny, the little girl, sat with her new best friend beside her with a miniature dinner set she'd taken from her other toys.

"Please give Arty some chicken too!" she asked, as she straightened out Arty's Christmas suit. Red and white candy cane stripes down his arms and legs matched the neat little bow on his chest. Arty didn't like the bow too much, but it made Jenny happy, so the robot could hardly complain.

"I hope you have a merry Christmas, Mom and Dad," Jenny said, then turned to the robot. "And you too, Arty."

"You know," said Arty in his little robot language that only Jenny could understand, "I think it's going to be a perfect Christmas."

And it was.

J. T. MORIARTY

J. T. Moriarty is too busy to write a bio himself, between uni, child-bot rearing, cat juggling, writing, editing, walking in the Blue Mountains, bicycling, editing, re-editing, finding some cheap glue to keep himself stuck to his seat, drinking coffee — no, no, that coffee...it wasn't strong enough — cleaning the house, moving the cats off the keyboard, planning holidays, planning too many books at once, canceling those holidays, chilling to ambient vibes, AND writing for anthologies, so we've opted for this as a press release/mission statement instead:

'Please send help.'

-J. T. Moriarty

P.S. We felt we should add that Moriarty writes fantasy, science fiction, and creative drama. This is the fourth anthology he has been in.

His debut series 'The Full Life of a Robot' needs your care and attention.

facebook.com/jaytea.moriarty.3

instagram.com/jtmoriartywriter

NAUGHTY AND NICE

A. A. WARNE

E mma opened the door just enough to stick her head out and checked to see if the coast was clear. Half a dozen random faces lurked along the corridor but thankfully, no one she recognized. She popped out of the closet and shut the door behind her.

The dangling KEEP OUT sign banged against the wood, and she planted her hand against it, trying to cover her tracks.

"What were *you* doing in there?"

Jumping, she swung around to face her best friend. "Nothing!"

Benny's lips flattened into a line, and he raised an eyebrow. "I don't believe you."

Letting out a huge sigh, she turned her back to him and pressed a little box to her stomach so he couldn't see. "I don't care," she said, taking off down the corridor, "because you never believe me!"

He trailed behind her, clutching his bag's strap where it draped over one shoulder. "It's not like you give me enough reason to."

She stopped dead in her tracks, turned, and glared. "What's that supposed to mean?"

Half stumbling back, he gulped. "Emma!" He cowered, conscious of the hallway filling up with students who were rushing to their next class. He closed the distance between them and whispered, "You always get me into trouble."

Squinting her angry eyes at him, she huffed, "I never!" then turned into the busy crowd and stomped off toward the dorm rooms.

"Really?" he huffed. "Then what's that in your hands?"

"Nuffin!" she moaned.

"See. You did it again!" He ran after her and leaned out, placing a hand on her shoulder. "Slow down, would you?"

"Nope!" she sulked. "You're ruining the surprise!"

"Huh?" He didn't ease up but instead caught up to her and got in her way.

"Is that what this attitude is about?" he winked toward the box. Her eyes darted both ways, and then she nodded.

"I thought we weren't giving each other presents."

"Well..." she paused, taking in deep breaths. "Maybe I changed my mind."

"Oh, crap," said Benny. "Because... I didn't."

"That's okay," she said, reaching for his hand. "Let's go."

"Wait. Where?"

"My room. You can open it now."

"Hold on!" he protested, but she yanked his hand, and he was on the move, dragging behind her fast. "What were you doing in the store room?"

"Shush!" she yelled at him.

Benny couldn't help but follow her lead. She often ran around him in circles, getting him into all sorts of trouble while she remained pure and innocent. If they hadn't been best friends since preschool, he'd probably move on to someone who wasn't so daring. But their friendship had survived every twist and turn life threw at them. Nothing could tear them apart now.

"Good!" Emma said, stomping into the middle of her room. "Julie isn't back yet."

Benny lingered. He liked Julie, but Julie didn't like Benny in their room and often made such a fuss that if she was doing it on stage, she would have won awards.

"Did you lock the door?" Emma asked.

"For what!"

"Just do it. And hurry up." Emma crossed her legs and placed the box before her. "Come on, sit down already. I'm excited."

"Can you breathe for a moment, please?" Benny locked the door and sat down on the rug, crossing his legs to match Emma. "You're giving me whiplash."

"No," she laughed. "I'm giving you a Christmas present."

"Why can't it wait?"

"Another week? That's too long!"

Benny smirked. "Oh, I forgot. You're not one with patience."

She flicked the back of her hand across his shoulder and then shoved the present into his hands. "Open it."

Taking the box carefully, he turned it over and around in his hands for a closer look.

Emma inched forward, eyes wide and hungry.

He leaned back and stared at her. "You didn't wrap this."

"Clearly, it's a box."

"A dusty box!" He held it back out to her. "You stole this from the cabinet, didn't you?"

Shaking her head, she looked him dead in the eyes. "I cross my heart and promise you that this present is from me." She motioned with her hand to mimic the actions of her words.

Squinting his eyes, he glared at her. "I can't tell if you're lying to me."

"What! Why wouldn't you believe me?" she retorted.

"I want to, but…"

"Then open it! The suspense is killing me!"

"Because you don't know what's inside?" He smirked, catching her like a fly in his carefully-worded web. It was only a matter of time before she hooked herself up.

She let out a big breath, clearly calming herself, and slowly handed the box to him. "Benny. You are my favorite human and my only bestest friend in the world. Merry Christmas."

He looked at the box and then back to her. His fingertips inched closer to the suspicious present, hesitating for just a moment, but he pressed on because he caught a glimpse of her big doe-eyes. There were only so many times he could say no to her. "Thank you," he said quietly. "But I have a feeling I will regret this."

Placing the box gently on the floor, he stuck his fingernail in the gap and pulled back the dusty, cardboard lid.

A twist of black light sprang from the box and spiraled upward and outward, bursting through the bedroom.

They flopped backward onto the carpet, lowering themselves to the ground to give the weird tornado space.

Then, with a zip, it disappeared through the closed door.

Benny and Emma quickly sat back up and froze, taking a moment to catch their breath.

"What was that?" Benny whispered.

Emma shook her head without answer, and they both leaned forward and banged their heads together trying to look inside the box.

"Is that..." Benny started before trailing off. "Coal?" He looked up and glared at her.

"Are you asking *me*?" Emma cleared her throat. "Yes. I mean, no!"

Groaning, he reached inside and picked it up. "Umm, why would you give me coal?" he asked as they exchanged curious stares.

"Umm..." Emma's eyes went to the ceiling like she would find the answer up there. But before she found one, a death-defying scream sounded from the corridor.

Benny jumped as Emma grabbed the coal and shoved it back into the box and slid it beneath her bed.

"What was that?" Benny asked, getting to his feet and following the heart-crushing sound.

The scream was followed by another as they were met with a chorus of chaos.

"Something's going on." Emma rushed up behind Benny.

He unlocked the door, and they looked outside. Students were running up and down the corridor.

"Don't go outside," yelled a boy.

A girl stood to the side, sobbing, as something in her hand disintegrated into black dust. She looked up and saw them at the door. "Someone hexed us."

Benny slammed the door shut.

"Has everyone lost their minds?" Emma asked.

"What *was* that?" Benny breathed hard.

"Crazy people —"

He cut her off. "No, Emma, be serious. What was that black tornado thing when I opened the box?"

She shrugged and went for her bed, but he grabbed her hand and stopped her.

"What if that thing just caused everyone out there —" He paused.

She finished the sentence for him. "To go crazy?"

"What if it hurt them!" he corrected her.

"I'm sure after a good night's sleep they'll be fine."

Benny ran to the window. "Look!" He pointed toward the clouds where the school's protector, a dragon, breathed fire over the gates. "I haven't seen that before."

"We've never been under attack before."

"Yeah, but —"

"Emma!" he yelled.

"What?" She shrugged. "It's not my fault."

They looked out the window and noticed that the school's teachers were wrestling with the gates, trying to force them closed. On the other side were hundreds of deer, pushing their way through. The dragon dipped down, picked some up, and threw them back out beyond the gates.

"That's weird," she murmured. "Why are the deer setting off the alarms?"

Benny glared at her, "Because maybe everything in the corridor just turned to coal."

She ran back to the box and pulled it out from beneath the bed. "I didn't know," she admitted with a hint of fear.

Before he could say anything, the door burst open, and Emma's roommate, Julie, burst in.

Julie paused in horror at the sight of Benny in her room. "You're not allowed in here, remember?" she said.

"I'm just leaving," he said, heading for the door.

"I wouldn't go out there," Julie said, flopping down onto her bed and bursting into tears. "Christmas is ruined!"

"What happened?"

"I was doing my Christmas party duties and wrapping all the presents, and all of a sudden, there was this gust of wind, and the presents all turned to black lumps of coal." She moaned and wiped her tears. "I panicked and touched them, and then the coal turned to dust."

Benny and Emma exchanged glances.

Julie rolled over, burying her face in the pillow.

Pressing his lips into her ear so only Emma could hear, Benny whispered, "We need to get out of here."

"And go where?"

"To get help."

"The teachers have got this," she whispered back. "It's fine."

Julie rolled over and cried again. "And you know what happened next!"

"Wait. That wasn't the last of it?" Benny's eyes went even wilder.

"Deer ran into the hall and started ripping open all of the

presents—every single one that I just wrapped! They tore it apart. There's nothing left! Nothing!"

Emma scratched her head. "Deer? That's weird."

"They eat coal, and what's trying to get into the school right now?" He gave her the look.

She bit the inside of her mouth, trying to look innocent.

Benny grabbed Emma's arm and pulled her out the door and into the chaotic corridor. Kids ran in each direction, and they had to duck out of everyone's way.

Emma pressed herself against the wall and refused to budge. "I don't care where you're going, but I'm staying here."

"We did this, so we are going to fix it!"

"Why are you pulling me into this? It was your present!"

"Emma!"

She stood her ground and shrugged her shoulders.

He snatched the box from her and raised his voice. "Sometimes, you can be the worst!"

She gawked. "That's not very nice."

"I'm always nice to you, and you did this to me. You can come and help me fix Christmas, or you can go in to your roommate and tell her how it was you who did all this."

He turned and ran into the chaos, leaving her there to watch him go.

"Fine!" she yelled after him, but for the first time, he didn't stop and turn back to get her.

Her stomach sunk.

"Are you coming back?" she yelled, but her voice disappeared into the madness, and then she couldn't see him.

"Benny!" she screamed. But still, he was gone.

She stood there listening to her heartbeat, wondering what to do. She could go inside and cry next to Julie or she could run and hide and pretend she didn't have a hand in it.

But why couldn't she just have left that box inside the closet where she found it? She could have pinched herself.

Stomping her foot, she pushed forward, darting around

anyone who got in her way. "Move!" she ordered, not caring that anyone was having the worst day themselves. She needed to catch up with Benny, then grab the box and put it back in the closet where she found it.

That would solve every problem so she could wash her hands of this terrible day.

"Benny?" she called out as she ran through all the corridors toward his room. She opened the door and found it empty.

"Where are you!" she yelled and stomped her foot.

Thinking, she tried to work out where he would go. She was, after all, his bestest friend in the entire world. She would be the one with the answer.

Her shoulders slumped.

He would have gone straight to the gates and told the teachers. Reluctantly, she stomped to the main hallway and found a crowd of students gawking through the glass doors.

"Move," she ordered them, and they parted ways.

"You're not going out there, are you?" one kid asked her.

She rolled her eyes at him and laughed. "Why? You're too scared to?"

He inched backward. "Your funeral!"

Beneath her breath, she whispered, "Oh, I know," and moved to the front of the crowd.

Through the glass door, she saw Benny standing in the middle of the courtyard speaking to Principal Scout.

Emma and the principal hadn't seen eye-to-eye in some time, so Emma did her best to avoid the domineering woman. Who was she to argue with authority at every conversation? But now, Benny was facing her alone, and she was behind the protection of the glass front doors.

Placing her hand firmly on the handle, she froze.

A voice behind her said, "You don't want to do that!"

"Don't tell me what I know." She ignored every gut feeling and twisted the knob, letting the cool, fresh air pour in.

Benny was pleading with Principal Scout. "I didn't know,"

he said. "I mean, I've never heard of such magic. Can it be undone?"

The dragon circled overhead while Emma inched her way closer to Benny and stood behind him.

"That depends," Principal Scout said. "Are you ready to give me the truth?"

Benny nodded. "Yes, Ma'am."

"Where did you get the box from?"

"I…" Benny paused and gulped, then spoke with a firmer voice. "I found it."

If Principal Scout wasn't staring at both of them, Emma would have rolled her eyes. Benny wasn't a liar, he always left Emma to take charge when they needed a white fib or two.

Principal Scout lifted her hand into the air and made a circle.

The dragon took off into the distance, circled back, and landed beside her. Its wingspan was so vast that each swoop lifted every pebble and stone, sending them hurtling toward Emma and Benny and coating them in dust.

"Now, it's important you don't move."

They froze.

The dragon walked on its hind legs, marching straight toward Benny.

"See, dragons are a very intelligent species," Principal Scout said. "It doesn't matter what words you say because they do not hear our language like we do. But they do listen to our heartbeat—the way it pulsates through our veins—and how our muscles react to that rhythm."

Benny's fingers locked on the box. His neck went stiff, and he held his breath.

"Now, if someone isn't truthful to themselves, a dragon will tell."

His eyes firmly locked on Principal Scout, Benny didn't see the fire in the dragon's eyes. "What does that have to do with this box?"

"Great question, Benjamin."

Instantly, his shoulders went up to his ears and his head jerked to the side. He hated being called by that name.

The dragon reacted to his fast movements, inching closer and snarling at him.

"See," Principal Scout continued like the dragon wasn't licking his lips and about to eat Benny. "Rhythms and heartbeats are very much like coal and deer. They go together nicely, because what's a heartbeat without a rhythm?"

"I don't get it."

"Deer do love coal. And dragons do love to eat liars." The principal smiled devilishly.

Benny raised his voice. "But—"

Emma placed a hand on his shoulder.

The dragon ran forward and straight past Benny, stopping barely an inch from Emma's nose.

"Oh," Principal Scout said elegantly, "there's one now."

The dragon huffed out a meaty breath, covering Emma's face and blowing back her hair.

"Emma?" Benny twisted around, looking surprised she was there.

"Do you have something to say?" Principal Scout came over and placed a hand on the dragon's head.

"I...um..." Emma quivered under the glares of Benny, Principal Scout, and the dragon. "Not really."

Benny slumped again.

She saw the pain in his eyes and stood up straight. "It was me. I'm the problem. I broke into the closet on the fifth floor in the East block and found this box."

"East block, did you say? And why would you do such a thing?"

"I don't know."

"But surely you do know."

"I was bored. And I got in trouble in Science again so I snuck out looking for something to do."

"Miss Emma you are a very bright young girl, and my dragon is very hungry. Is that all you want to say?"

She turned back to Benny. "I really want to say I'm sorry. I don't know why I get you into so much trouble."

Benny smiled. "You're admitting it?"

She nodded. "Sometimes I don't know what's wrong with me."

"Oh, a lot," he added.

She smacked him on the arm. "That's not fair."

"You getting me in trouble every day isn't fair. I never do anything to you!"

Hanging her head, she lowered her voice. "I know."

"Right," Principal Scout clapped her hands. "We have a mess to clean up."

Benny held out the box to Principal Scout who backed away and shook her head.

"Oh no, dear boy, that now belongs to you."

"What?"

"I hid that thing to get rid of it years ago. I'm surprised no one else found it sooner."

"What!" Benny raised his voice.

"Think of it as my Christmas present to you. Now you get to hide it, and hopefully, you'll do better than I did."

"Isn't this thing a hex?"

Principal Scout half-shrugged one shoulder. "Sure, you can say that, but only to those who open it."

"But everyone's gifts have turned to coal."

"And then if you touch the coal, it turns to dust," Emma added.

"Oh, that's a silly trick I put on the box so I would know when someone had opened it." Principal Scout held up her finger, and the tip glowed like starlight. "I call back the power of coal."

The light on the tip of her finger glowed even brighter, and a swirl of dark mist moved over the entire school, racing toward the starlight. It created a tornado overhead and sunk into the bright light, burning and dissipating on impact.

"So, that was all a spell then?"

Principal Scout nodded. "Clever, wasn't it?"

"And the deer? Why did you create that?"

"Oh, that's the unfortunate thing about magic. Sometimes, not even I can predict the consequences." She turned her head the other way, peering out the gates. "Run along deer," she leaned in and kissed the dragon on the forehead. "Go and have some fun." The dragon took the orders and flew straight up into the sky. "I hope you two learned your lesson."

"Sort of?" Benny said in a confused tone.

"Nope," Emma added.

Principal Scout laughed. "Well, I'll let you in on a secret then." She curled a finger for them to lean forward, and as they did, she whispered, "Never sacrifice true friendship." She looked up and winked at the dragon.

Benny and Emma exchanged looks.

"I can live with that," Benny said.

"Me too."

Principal Scout walked toward the glass front doors.

"Oh, wait a sec," Emma yelled out, catching the principal's attention. "What about everyone's presents?"

Pulling a face, Principal Scout spoke quietly. "No more will turn to coal, but between us, the ones that did... Well, there's no turning that back."

Benny gasped. "That's horrible!"

"Well, perhaps..." Principal Scout added, looking over her shoulder at the watching students still glaring through the doors. "Perhaps that's this year's lesson for everyone else."

Emma watched her enter the doors and move the students along. As soon as the door closed, Emma leaned into Benny. "Good thing we didn't get each other presents this year."

"Oh, with your record, we're never giving each other presents *ever* again!"

A. A. WARNE

I'm a speculative fiction wizard; I bend genres.

I write passionate characters in problematic worlds, exploring impossible situations while enduring an emotional kick.

When I'm not writing, I'm chasing after three wild children and two seriously naughty dogs in the sub-tropical climate of Rockhampton, Queensland, in Australia.

www.aawarne.com

facebook.com/aawarne

x.com/aawarne

instagram.com/aawarne

amazon.com/stores/A.-A.-Warne/author/B07Q819NCB

bookbub.com/profile/a-a-warne

goodreads.com/aawarne

linkedin.com/in/aawarne

NOVA STELLARUM

M.J.J. MORI

*S*tarlight—it's what we're all made of. The scattered dust of long-dead stars is deeply embedded in our bones and flows through our pulsing veins. Each of those infinitesimal specks of dust contains an even smaller spark of starlight, left over from the intense fusion that churns the hearts of each solar godhead. And there is a way, however difficult, to focus that deepest darkest patina of our life, to hone that star stuff and concentrate it to our will. It took a long time, but I found the way and stepped into a larger world.

Only ten minutes after I'd finally cracked the method of starlight control, a tall, blonde lady wearing dark red beneath a black leather jacket and holding an old, leather-bound book appeared in my darkened lounge room, standing between the three-seater and armchair and staring intensely at me.

Then she looked around, unimpressed. "Why are all the lights off?" Only a small, weak lamp in the corner provided any light.

Her sudden presence and beauty struck me speechless. I held my hands up and shook my head.

"Who are you?" she demanded, unwinding her bright-red scarf from around her neck.

I smiled foolishly. "I'm Dylan."

She shook her head dismissively. "I don't care about your name. What is your family branch?"

No idea. I shrugged. "Umm, the Joneses?"

"Right," she replied, annoyed. "Do *the Joneses* possess the command of starlight?" She waved her book before her, a large jewel in its cover glowing ever-so-slightly blue.

"Ah, nope," I replied. "Well, not to my knowledge. Maybe Uncle Chugg."

She stepped forward, taking my hands and examining them like a scientist. "Maybe it's a false positive."

Up close she was even more beautiful, and I knew I had to pull myself together. I took her hands in mine and looked deeply into her eyes. "There's nothing false about this meet-cute," I purred, excited to seize the moment while also cringing inside.

She snatched her hands out of mine, eyes flaring.

"You know, ah, just saying," I stammered.

"Look, *Dylan*, you are on the edge of something you cannot begin to comprehend." She walked away from me and around the lounge room, her tall, leather boots clicking on the wooden floorboards and distaste crossing her face as she took in the authentic shabby-chic of my secondhand furniture. "There's a world inside the one you know. Very dangerous, very old." She stopped and turned toward me, her short, tartan skirt spinning around her, and resumed studying me. "We just received an alarm that you gained the power of starlight control. Do you know what I'm talking about?"

"You mean this?" I asked and shot a small blast of white-blue light from my fingertips across the room into my classic jukebox. It burst to life, merrily singing *Jingle Bell Rock*.

She groaned. "Okay, there goes the rest of my day. Come with me."

. . .

Leading us out of my old townhouse into the front garden, she inspected me from the top down, frowning. "Surely you can't do much more than that?"

I shook my head. "Haven't had time to try anything else yet,"

She wrapped her red scarf back around her neck. "Okay, what we're about to do is called travelating. It is quite tricky, at least the first few times, so you'll have to let me help you." She offered me her hand then snatched it back as I reached out for it. "This is *not* the beginning of a beautiful friendship," she said firmly.

I grimaced. "Yeah, I got that."

"Okay," she said, giving me her hand. "Take a deep breath and try to relax as much as possible. In your mind, imagine yourself as liquid starlight. That should help, and I'll do the rest."

She tensed up to do something, then paused and muttered, "This'll either work or instantly kill you."

"Wait, what?"

"I've never seen it actually do that. Don't worry about it. Just had a legal obligation to inform you." She winked.

"Umm, well, what are we waiting for?" I said with false bravado.

"I guess if it's the latter, you'll never know," she said, smirking. "Let's go."

With second-thoughts growing, I did as she instructed. I quickly breathed in and imagined myself starlight, my body all made of the same stuff that had shot out of my fingers. Then, for a few moments, it felt like I became starlight, a stream of lightning forking up into the sky and across the star-filled night and down onto the ice-covered ground. And suddenly, I was standing beside her just as I had been before, and she was the same—tense and holding my hand. Then she relaxed and inspected me with concern. "Hello? You still in there?"

I didn't move, except to blink a few times and look around. "I think so. Yes. Maybe." We were the same, but the whole world had changed. We were standing in a broad, night-blue field that stretched away to the horizon, punctuated with knolls and groves of trees. I relaxed and turned to her. "Yep, one hundred."

"Well, that's a relief. Some people never come back whole, or in any way at all, on their first travelation."

"Oh, you weren't joking," I said brusquely, my stomach grumbling. "I might have really died?"

She frowned. "I don't know you," she explained, annoyed. "If it'd been for the worse, it'd actually make my day easier. I'd fill out a form about what happened and get on with it. But now that you're here and reasonably present, I'll have to admit you and set you up with a trainer."

My stomach rumbled more urgently. "What? Where?"

She led the way into the blue field and, facing me, stood resplendent in her red top and scarf and red tartan skirt, long blonde locks flowing down over her black, leather coat. "Here, at the Hotelier Lodge."

She began quietly chanting. Her right hand glowed with a spark of bright blue light as she raised it over the scene, and the leather-bound book similarly glowed in her left hand. Atop the blue fields behind her, a tall, ornate gate appeared like a blanket had been pulled away, and behind that emerged a path flanked with trees leading to a dark mansion, almost a castle in its stature and style. "We will teach you the ways of starlight control."

The house and trees were swathed in a rainbow of multi-colored fairy lights. Snowflakes fell from the sky and swept through the corners of the fenced yard. I smiled while holding my stomach, then groaned while almost doubling over.

"Don't worry about that," she said without looking. "It's just the squitts."

My stomach felt like it was doing backflips. "The what?"

"An aftereffect of your first travelation. It'll pass."

"It sure feels like everything will pass."

She rolled her eyes. "I'm not going into much detail, but when we travelate for the first time, *everything* is disturbed. It'll take time for it to settle back down, one way or another. Come on, let's get out of the cold."

"Cold?" In my excitement, I'd failed to notice the chunks of snow littering the area. I shivered.

She turned and walked through the gates and along the path toward the foreboding house. I straightened as much as I could and followed her. Each step felt better, and by the time I reached the commanding front entrance—an enclosure surrounded by columns and carved stone—the stomach pain had disappeared, though I still felt anything but normal. Something magical was happening; something I'd never dreamed of in a million years.

My guide flashed her hand in front of a circular panel on the door and stood back.

"Is this…where Santa lives?" I asked.

"What? Of course not," she replied. "Now be quiet."

A moment later, the door's circular panel dissipated and a face appeared. "Hello?" it said in a long drawn-out question.

"Open up, Latch," she said, tapping her book on her leg. "It's me."

"Who's me?" the face asked.

She scowled and brushed a glowing finger across the centre of the clear panel. The face grunted, swearing. "Okay, Angelar!" it shouted. "No need for theatrics!" The panel clouded and the door opened.

"Every. Single. Time," she said and swept into the lodge.

I halted, suddenly aware that this was one of those thresholds of my life, literal and metaphorical. I could turn around, I thought, right now, and go back to my life and not get involved with whatever madness was going on behind this tall, wide, steel-bound wooden door. Back to my crummy, boring, run-of-the-mill life. Which had driven me to believe in the possibility of unlikely star magic. To the point that I'd spent hundreds of painful hours trying to make it work. Only to find out this? I snapped with my right hand, and the spark it procured from the crack of my fingers warmed my heart. I eagerly stepped through the door.

The entryway was wide and led into an enormous foyer packed with tall marble statues of clearly important people, all holding a book similar to Angelar's. I walked behind Angelar along a blue rug laid through the center of the collection. On the other side of the room, opposite the front door of the lodge, was an ornate desk, and behind the desk sat two elderly people. In front of each of them lay a very large book. The effect was a mirror reflection, except that one was male and one was female.

They watched Angelar approach but said nothing.

"Gurty. Burty," she said, nodding to each in turn by way of greeting. "At the request of Hayer, here is a new recruit. He has demonstrated *nova stellarum fluxus*. Please put him through to education." She elbowed me in the arm, and I stepped forward.

"Name?" asked the old lady.

"Dylan."

She glared at me, wrinkled eyes alert. "Family name".

"Jones."

She opened the book in front of her and turned the pages until she found the one she wanted and then ran a finger down the listings. "Hmm," she muttered and turned to the old man.

He repeated the procedure precisely, then turned back to his counterpart and shook his head once.

"He is not listed," Gurty announced. "There has been a mistake."

Angelar sighed. "I assure you, he's capable. I saw it myself."

The old man leaned forward and stared at me. "Who taught you?"

"No one. I figured it out myself," I explained.

The old lady leaned forward. "What gave you the idea to try? A family member?"

"It was discussed in an old magazine I found in a dumpster behind the public library," I explained.

Angelar looked at me sideways.

"An old seeking key," said Burty. "We don't have many out there now."

"Indeed," said Gurty, squinting with thought.

"You were in a dumpster?" asked Angelar, unimpressed.

"Well, you know, not right inside it," I said.

"What were you looking for?" asked Gurty.

"Not lunch, I hope," snarked Angelar.

"I'm not sure," I replied to Gurty, ignoring Angelar. "I was taking a shortcut behind the library and spotted a big stack of books in the bin and was struck with the idea there might be something good in there. Like I was suddenly compelled to check."

"That settles it then," said Burty. "The seeking key might have been hidden on a shelf in that library for many years."

"Righto," said Angelar. "I'm off."

"Not so fast," said Gurty. "How could a seeking key in a very public library not find a nascent user for that long?"

"Well, we know for sure he's not in the books," said Burty, thumping the top of his open book with a heavy pointer finger. "He can't stay here."

"It's not my problem," asserted Angelar and started walking away from them. "Good knowing you," she said to me with a wave.

"What does that mean?" I asked, following her.

She turned and stopped me. "Hey, you stay here. The twins will sort you out."

The twins glanced at each other and sighed. "It's true."

A spark of dread flickered down my neck. I really wasn't welcome. "That's okay," I said urgently, raising my hands. "I can make my own way home." I backed toward the front door.

Angelar stood by and watched as the aged twins stood up and raised their hands toward me. "You'll have to come with us," said the old man. His fingers sparkled.

I blanched. "No, it's fine. I can see myself out."

The twins moved as one, throwing white lines of light energy from their hands at me. But I was quick, and with determination thought of the snowy world outside and my body as a river of electricity. It worked well enough that my body turned translucent and the lines of energy from the twins passed through without contact. They withdrew the lines of energy and I re-solidified. "Damn it," I spat and ran across the foyer behind the large statues. "What are you doing?" I shouted.

"Come back," called Burty. "We need to secure you while we figure out what to do."

I didn't trust them.

"This isn't going to work," said Angelar to the twins as she watched from nearby with her arms crossed.

"Stay out of it," said Gurty. "I thought you said you were leaving?"

"I'm not coming back," I shouted, looking around the foyer for an escape.

The twins walked around the desk and toward the statues where I hid. Their hands glowed with starlight energy.

"You stay back now," I shouted lamely. "I'm warning you." Above the twins, I saw a large chandelier, and taking a chance flicked a bolt at it from my fingertips. The chandelier rocked in its place, staying firmly attached to the ceiling. The twins ran back behind their desks.

"Amateurs," muttered Angelar, shaking her head. She travelated behind me, grabbed me in a bear hug, and said, "You can't travelate directly out of the lodge. Come with me."

The tone in her voice assured me, and sensing her starting to travelate, I again relaxed and turned to light.

We appeared on the other side of the room in front of the main entrance, and we ran outside.

Angelar swore as the door slammed shut behind her. "Now I'm in for it," she shouted.

"Sorry?" I said, stumbling. "I'm not sure what's going on."

"It's not your fault," she said, sighing as she led me away behind some dark-green fir trees lit with fairy lights of red, green, and blue. "You weren't in the book. That's a problem. But those two old fools were ridiculous. You're clearly not a threat to the Hostel."

"Well, I might be," I said, relaxing. "I mean, I can do this." I snapped my sparking fingers.

"Nope, not even close," said Angelar, distracted by a snowflake that landed on her nose.

"Maybe."

"Not for a second."

"I could…"

"Uh-huh," she said, pulling a silly face then growing serious. "Look, Dylan, I can see you're a nice enough guy. The thing is, you've visited the Hostel now. You know about it, and that's a problem if you're not welcome here." Angelar sighed with the weight of a wrecked day. "Only members are supposed to know about it. I wouldn't have taken you directly, but the order I got from the top was to pick you up and take you there."

"Who sent the order?"

"Hayar, Lord Master of the Hostel. But he would know if you weren't in the books already."

"How?"

"He writes them."

"Ah," I said, feeling deflated. "Maybe I can just go home?"

"Not a good idea. They'll be looking for you soon. Those two are slow, so we have a few minutes, but they are not to be underestimated. They are very powerful when motivated. We have to get moving and figure this out."

"Where, then?"

Angelar looked at me in thought. "New starlight seldom emerges in isolation. Who was that family member you mentioned that might have light powers?"

"Uncle Chugg?"

"Yeah, him. Let's check him out."

"That was a joke," I said. "He's a joke. Like, the family clown."

"Sure," replied Angelar, shrugging, "but I've seen stranger things. Where is he?"

As it was Christmastime, there would only be one place to find him. "At the Village Square in Baringdonton."

"How're your guts?"

"Hungry and courageous," I said with a grin. "In that order."

"I mean we've got to travelate again," she explained. "As in, properly. Further than across the room."

"Ah. Did you see? I almost travelated when they tried lassoing me."

"Yeah, pretty good for a *novus*," she said impressed. "Okay, let's go." She held out her hand.

I held it and breathed out, long and deep, relaxing, conceptualizing liquid lightning, and the world momentarily turned into the surface of a lake, and then we stood in the middle of a wide village square, snow-dusted and decorated with long lines of tinsel and lights between buildings and bows on doorways and giant gift boxes stacked in corners. Centered among it all was a tall Christmas tree holding snow and shining spheres and more tinsel and topped with a large, gilt-gold star.

"Your uncle is around here somewhere then?" asked Angelar, looking around.

"Yeah," I replied. "He's, ah, over there." I pointed to a small crowd surrounding a Christmas display housing Santa and his helpers and kids taking photos.

As we walked over, Angelar tried to figure out who in the crowd he was. "The man with the small boy in blue?"

"Nope."

"Hmm, the older man smoking the pipe?"

"Guess again."

Her eyes landed on the star of the show, and she laughed. "Oh, surely not."

"I'm afraid so."

I looked at Uncle Chugg, sitting there in Santa's tall, wooden chair, surrounded by kids and dressed in the red felt and white, fur-lined suit of Santa Claus. It seemed he was having a good time, as were the children. He really did seem to care as they told him what they wanted for Christmas. Cameras clicked, and the happy kids left Santa's workshop and a new batch shuffled in and the process repeated. After a couple sets of children, Uncle Chugg looked up and spotted me, giving me a nod and a short wave. I smiled and nodded back, and he waved me over. I shook my head, but he was insistent.

"Wait a moment," I told Angelar and walked over to where I could talk with him without entering the workshop. Yet again, he indicated I should draw closer, and I uncomfortably scrambled over the rope fence near him and leaned in.

"What are you doing with her?" he asked, eyes suddenly intense upon me. Some children approached, but he curtly held up his hand for them to wait.

I was a bit surprised by his question. "Who?" I asked and glanced over at Angelar. "You mean her?"

He was studying me now. "Oh…" he muttered and grinned

at me. "Yes, you've finally figured it all out." He winked his sparkling eyes.

Uncle Chugg wasn't just an old weirdo, like the family made him out to be. Clearly, he knew exactly what I was in the middle of, but I played dumb because I wanted to hear it from him.

"Uh, what are you talking about, Uncle?"

"That broad you're with," he said, thumbing in Angelar's general direction. "Where'd you pick her up?"

"She's an old friend," I said.

"Bull-dust," he blurted. "I know her. She's big trouble."

"What? *Her?*"

"Let me guess—you've never seen her before this evening?"

My expression must have given it away.

"You figured out how to use your starlight control, and then bang, a few minutes later, she turns up?"

The hateful look in his eye warned me not to say much.

He stood up, and he turned back into St. Nick with jolly grin and announced to all the children in a treacle voice that Santa was taking a break. Then he grabbed my arm and walked me over toward Angelar. "Don't worry," he said into my ear. "We're family. I've got your back."

I waved at Angelar, and as she started walking over to us through the bustling holiday crowd, I felt Uncle Chugg's grip on my arm slowly tighten to the point of pain. I also noticed he was walking more behind me, rather than at my side.

Angelar stopped a couple of strides away and nodded at me. "Angelar, this is Uncle Chugg," I said.

"Nice to meet you," she said. "Dylan tells me you're a notable family member."

"Of course I am," replied Chugg. "But who you are and why you might be so interested in my nephew is my primary interest." His eyes under the Santa hat were locked onto her, and the white beard and mustache covering his mouth jiggled as he spoke.

"Dylan," began Angelar, but as she said this, her eyes grew startled, and she looked around at the families crowding the village square. "Dylan shows much promise with starlight control," she stated clearly. "But you already know that, don't you?" She slowly assumed a ready position.

Uncle Chugg laughed gruffly. "Took your time, girl," he snarled.

Angelar raised her right hand toward him, a hint of light playing between her fingers. "You're lucky this Square is not a good place for exchanging our true sentiments."

"You have no such luck!" growled Chugg, and he shoved me toward her and leaped to the right. The white beam of light that spun out of his flickering hand curved around me and scalded her left arm. Angelar barely flinched and darted away into the crowd.

I fell to the ground but jumped up quickly, confused about who to follow. Nothing but the crowd suddenly surrounded me, a flighty mess of holiday cheer silenced and looking at me.

A young man asked if I was okay. "What was that about?"

I made a booze-drinking action with my hand and shook my head. He laughed and disappeared into the crowd, which quickly resumed its festive cheer. Without another moment's thought, I followed after Angelar.

Chugg found me first. I felt his iron grip grasp my arm once more. "Well done, boy," he said sweetly. "You've played your part perfectly."

"What are you talking about, you old fool?" I said. My estimation of Uncle Chugg had plummeted from cool, weird uncle to raving lunatic. Who could fire magic from their hands at will.

I stopped, shook off his hand, and faced him. The crowd bustled around us, oddly disinterested. "Who *are* you?"

Uncle Chugg stood tall and waved his glowing hand in a

wide circular motion over is head, sweeping away his Santa suit to reveal a dark and elaborate Victorian suit. "I am Robert Ross Knightly, ninety-ninth Lord of Lodge Mount Harton," he said with gravitas.

The crowd momentarily paused and cheered the free show. I smirked.

His hand sparkled and he leaned in close to me. "This is no joke, my boy. That woman you were with, she's one of the soldiers of Lodge Hotelier, the most evil and deceptive people."

"They seemed all right to me."

"Oh, you've met more than just her?" He firmly grasped my arm once more.

"I went there. Met the twins."

"Excellent," growled Chugg, and the world swam liquid.

A few moments later, Lodge Hotelier solidified before us. "Finally!" he exclaimed, letting me go. "Thanks to you, I've found it."

We stood at the place where I'd first seen the lodge earlier that evening. But that prior sense of excitement was replaced with dread. Something malevolent was in the air. "What are we doing here?"

Chugg walked toward the house, raised his hands slowly and widely, and began arcing forks of electricity up over his head. "Time for a little illumination!"

"Hey!" I shouted. "Stop!"

"Stay out this, boy," he bellowed, moving closer to the house.

A small spark of light cracked him in the back of this dark-leather cloak.

He turned on me and laughed at my shallow attack. "Little hero, hey? Don't you know? You're on my side, boy. We're in this together. All of this is built on blood!" He raised a hand toward me, palm outward, and I sensed deep within a magnetic force drawing me to my uncle. "You're a *Knightly*, too, underneath all that *Jones*. Help me destroy this lodge, and I'll bathe you well in glory."

I could feel that deep inside Uncle Chugg spoke the truth about our connection. But I wasn't about to help him destroy Lodge Hotelier. I'd done enough already by bringing him here.

I knew it was useless, but I started shooting light from my hands at him, flicking sparks as fast as I could.

His upheld hand smeared the air before him, seeming to create an invisible shield, and my attacks all dissipated in a shower of fading sparks. "Calm down, Dylan," he growled. "You're beginning to annoy me."

I faked to the left and shot one at him, then dove to the right as far as I could and shot a couple more, and one of my bolts singed his trim suit pants. In a flash of light, he suddenly sprang toward me, knocking me to the ground and standing over me with one of his feet on my chest.

"The only reason you're not dead already is our familial connection. But let me assure you, boy, sometimes that's just not enough." He reached down and placed his glowing hands around my head. "No one fires on me and gets away with it."

I struggled to free myself but my skull was split apart with an immense pain and the world seared with blue light. I tried changing into liquid but couldn't concentrate through the pain to do anything. I grabbed his legs to shove him over, but his stance was firm. "Nobody!" he shouted.

The world exploded with white light. His hands left my head, and he stepped back, letting me roll away.

Where he had just stood, now stood Angelar, her right hand raised and glowing like the sun, and in her left hand, her book wreathed in yellow flames.

"Begone, Lord Knightly," she commanded. "Profane this place no longer!"

My uncle only shook his head and laughed. "Time for a lesson in power, girl," he declared, and holding his hands toward Angelar, he bathed her in a pulsating force of dark light.

She held her flaming tome with both hands and a shield of golden flames surrounded her, pushing back the dark light. But it wasn't enough, and the flames began to flicker and falter under Uncle Chugg's onslaught.

On either side of her appeared the twins, their hands glowing brightly, and above them, levitating in the air, was an old gentleman I hadn't seen before. He wore a grand suit similar to that which my uncle had revealed at the Square.

Uncle Chugg assumed a defensive position, letting the dark light pulsating around Angelar fall away. "Lord Hayar, my old friend," he called. "Time has not been kind to you."

"I am no friend of yours," said Lord Hayar, and he snapped his finger at the enemy before his gates.

Uncle Chugg was surrounded by a glowing blue orb, and as he disappeared within it, he looked at me and snarled, "This isn't over yet."

Angelar helped me up from the snow as Lord Hayar alighted nearby and the twins approached. "Come inside," she said. "Your name's been found in the book."

I looked around and the rest of the group nodded toward me.

"Indeed, you have proven your mettle, Dylan," said Lord Hayer warmly.

"We have some eggnog on the stove," said the twins.

M.J.J. MORI

It is said that narrative is our chief sense-making tool. With this in mind, I seek to write stories that illuminate not only the world around us but the world that we find within. SF provides fertile grounds for such inquiries, whether it is a young girl seeking to live her dreams by befriending a giant or an old potions master wistfully recalling a lost love. How would you feel if you suddenly found you could channel the stardust running through your veins? What might a space traveler find at the fringes of time and space after leaving Earth billions of years before? Join me with a spirit of adventure as we set out from our cozy couches and explore new and exciting worlds. Godspeed!

www.mjjmori.com

 mastodon.social/mjjmori

STARLIGHT ETERNAL

MADILYNN DALE

Caroline Stars stood at her locker, pulling her books out for class. The Blizzard Blast Ball, being held Christmas Eve, hovered in the back of her mind. She still didn't have a date, and time was running out. She hoped Erick Morte, her all time crush, would ask her, but he was out of her league. Seniors never asked sophomores to attend the Ball, and he was one of the best wizards in the school. Why would he want to take someone like her? She wasn't even that pretty. Still, she wished it would happen.

She had to have a date for the ball. One didn't attend without one—it was unheard of! She couldn't ask someone herself, that was against the rules of the ball, and her closest guy friend had already asked someone. There had to be a way to get a date and go. It was unheard of for someone in her family to miss it. It was a family tradition to attend the ball if you were enrolled in the academy.

Rolling her eyes, she thought of all the stupid standards each student was required to follow to continue enrollment. Kingsley Academy was a special school specifically for witches, wizards, sorcerers, and the like. Many of the students, including herself, were following in their families' footsteps and continuing the family legacy at the academy.

Caroline's family was one of the founding members, so for her it wasn't an option to attend anywhere else. With the strength of the stars running through her veins, she would one day be required to hold a council position in the local coven and teach classes.

Frustrated, she slammed her locker closed, causing the holiday ornaments dangling above her head to crash together, jingling loudly. She sighed and rushed to class, only to be stopped by a large, shaggy, black dog.

"Oh," she exclaimed as she moved to the side, but its green eyes—glowing with power—followed her. It stepped in front of her and sat, its large tail thumping against the floor.

"You want me?"

Lifting its bushy chin, the dog revealed the small scroll held in its mouth. It hmphed as if responding to her question.

Caroline gasped as she finally recognized the dog as Erick's familiar. She stroked his head gently as she spoke. "Hey, big guy."

The dog dropped the scroll, and it unrolled at Caroline's feet.

Dearest Caroline,

Please do me the honor of attending the Blizzard Blast Ball with me.

Sincerely,

Erick Morte

"Well, that's unexpected." She picked the scroll up from the floor and held it to her chest.

Her heart raced, and she closed her eyes to send up a silent prayer to the goddess. Opening them, she smiled down at the dog. "Please tell your partner I said yes, big guy. I guess wishes do come true!"

The dog wagged its tail before bounding down the hall. Students moved out of his way as he went.

She twirled with the scroll held high above her head. It had happened! She had a way to go to the ball! And with the man of her dreams! She wouldn't be a disappointment. How though? Did the goddess truly grant her this gift?

Bouncing on the balls of her feet, she resumed walking to class with a smile plastered on her face. That small note had improved her entire day, maybe her entire week.

As she entered class, she ran to her usual table and slid into the chair beside Daisy. Caroline gushed to her best friend, "You're never going to believe what just happened!"

"Oh, tell me!" Daisy's eyes widened as she leaned toward Caroline.

"Well, I was at my locker when — "

The loudspeaker at the front of the room crackled loudly, interrupting their conversation. Caroline forced her excitement down as she pursed her lips and the room went silent.

"Attention students, it is with much sadness that I share the news of Sandy Townson. She was found dead in the woods last night."

Gasps and cries filled the room as Caroline sat back in her seat in shock. Her hand shot to her mouth as her eyes widened.

"We have grief counseling available for those who need it. At this time, though, I ask everyone to please join me in a moment of silence in remembrance of our friend."

The room was silent for several minutes, but Caroline's racing heart was loud in her ears. Time seemed to stand still as she closed her eyes to honor her late friend.

"Please continue your day as best you can. Thank you, students." The speaker crackled again, and the room burst into a loud frenzy.

Caroline hugged herself and looked at Daisy. "What do you think happened?"

Daisy lifted a shoulder. "I have no idea. I had dinner with her just last night. She didn't mention doing anything other than attending study group in the library. I can't believe it."

Caroline dropped her head into her hands. "Me either."

Clearing her throat at the front of the room, the teacher clapped her hands to get everyone's attention. With a shaky breath, she began teaching the class. Caroline did her best to focus on the lecture as thoughts of Sandy twirled through her head.

The rest of the day seemed to move by in a blur. The loss of her fellow classmate weighed heavily on Caroline. She wasn't that close to Sandy, but they had been lab partners a few times. She was a sweet girl. Rumors began to circle that she had been murdered.

Caroline could hardly believe it. She found it impossible that something like this would happen on campus. There weren't any with ill intent. Everyone had to pass a screening at the start of each semester. Several students had run away recently, but that was different from a murder.

As she walked toward the academy's massive library to spend a few hours meditating and studying, someone placed their hand on her shoulder, startling her from her thoughts. She whipped around, ready to cast a defensive spell, but stopped when she saw Erick standing there.

He held both hands up in a sign of peace. "Hey, sorry, I didn't mean to scare you. I called out your name."

"You did? I mean, hi."

"Are you okay?"

"Yes, you scared me a bit, but that's my fault. I was totally lost in thought. It's been a day. How are you?"

"I'm doing okay considering today's events. But hey, I wanted to spend some time with you." He smiled and shrugged a shoulder.

She scrunched up her nose and whispered, "Me too."

"And thanks for accepting my invitation to the Ball. It's crazy that it will be the night before Christmas, right?"

"It is, but my family celebrates on a different night so it

doesn't affect me much. I was headed to the library to study. Do you want to get one of the group rooms so we can talk without being scolded?"

"Yes. The librarian freaks me out. I still don't understand how a ghost is able to run the library. I wonder when she was actually alive?" Erick moved closer to Caroline, and they walked toward the library.

"My parents mentioned that she died back in the early 1900s when the school was founded. She took a liking to them."

"Oh, that's interesting," he said. "I guess you have a variety of knowledge since you're a descendant of the founding family?"

Caroline laughed. "You could say that. Where are you from, Erick?"

Caroline and Erick continued a steady conversation as they took up space in one of the group rooms. They chatted about their lives outside of the academy and the effects of the coven on family practices. They even decided on a color for the ball: silver, like the stars.

The night of the Ball finally arrived and campus was decorated in gorgeous shades of blue and gold. Caroline rested her hand in Erick's as they made their way along the snow-shoveled path to the assembly hall.

The two had grown close since the day Erick asked her to the ball. They shared Christmas gifts with each other, and Caroline was stunned at the gorgeous silver bracelet she was given. She smiled as she glanced down at her wrist. It matched her dress perfectly.

Lights twinkled overhead as they paused near the entrance to have their picture taken. Caroline loved that the school did such things. The beautiful event made up for the monotony of the school year.

Soon she was spinning in Erick's arms on the dance floor. They spent several hours dancing.

"Can we take a break and grab a drink? I feel a bit light-headed," Caroline yelled over the music, tugging at Erick's arm.

"That sounds great. Maybe we can get something and step outside for some fresh air? We could take a walk?"

"Oh, that sounds fantastic!" she said, heading toward the refreshments table.

A large, green punch bowl rested in the middle surrounded by dishes of food. A bubbling silver liquid sat within it, and as the teacher minding the table scooped it into glasses for the couple, it changed to a glowing violet.

Caroline nodded to the teacher as she grabbed two glasses and followed Erick outside.

"Oh! It's much colder out here than I realized." Caroline stopped at the rail, cradling her cup. She closed her eyes, and a gentle wind blew around them.

"It does. I didn't realize how warm it had gotten in there. Have I told you how gorgeous you are tonight in that silver dress?" Erick spun Caroline toward him and pulled her in for a kiss.

She blushed as she stepped back. "You just did."

"Let's walk this way. If we get away from the lights we can see how beautiful the sky is." He tugged at Caroline's wrist, and she let him lead her down the path.

As they walked, Caroline frequently turned her head to each side. The campus was decorated like something from a *Hallmark* Christmas movie. Trees were decorated with ornaments and mock presents sat at their bases.

Soon Erick led her off the sidewalk, toward the woods. The darkness was a huge contrast to the lights of the campus, but a full moon cast a gorgeous glow across the snow.

"Do we have much further to go before we stop to look at the stars? My heels aren't snow shoes."

"I promise it's right up here. I brought some blankets out earlier. I wanted to spend some time with you just gazing at the stars." Erick gave Caroline a charming smile.

"Okay." She moved in closer to him, hoping to share his warmth.

Five minutes later, the two entered a clearing lined with glowing candles. A star-filled sky and bright moon hovered above them. At the center of the clearing, a large blanket covered the snow. Piles of blankets sat next to a basket there, and Erick pulled Caroline over.

He encouraged her to sit down and wrapped her in a silver blanket. "This blanket almost matches your dress."

"It does," she exclaimed, fingering the fabric. "It's almost the color of starlight, like my magic."

"Really? You can see the color of your magic? I've only ever heard of a few people with the ability to see theirs."

"Well, yes, it's rare, but my family's magic is special. It only manifests in certain people in my family. My siblings and I all have it, but mine is much stronger. My mother tells me that it means I will do something huge one day. The fates supposedly have something planned for me."

"I wonder what that could be?" Erick tilted his head and wrapped her in another blanket. He tied it at the center in a strange knot before sitting next to her. "Now you should stay nice and warm."

Caroline laughed, "I guess you're right. It's almost impossible to move!"

"Would you like something to eat? Maybe some wine to drink?"

"Oh, how scandalous! You snuck wine out here? How did you even get your hands on some? I thought the resident advisors locked it up after their room raids last week?"

Erick chortled. "I do have my ways. When I want something, I always find a way to get it. So, would you like a glass?"

"What kind is it? I've never drank anything other than

what my mother has shared with me, and she drinks Cabernets."

Erick reached over to the large basket and pulled out a dark bottle. "It's a type of red blend. It's supposed to be sweet. I think you'll like it. I'm going to light some more candles as well. Maybe we can use our magic to warm ourselves better. I'll loosen your blanket for you first though."

Erick reached forward to loosen the knot to allow her to use her hands. He then reached into the basket to grab her a glass. Filling the glass for her, he gently set it in her hands, then set about pulling black candles from a bag. He lined them around the blanket in a circle, muttering something under his breath as he completed the task.

Sitting down next to Caroline, he asked, "Would you do the honors of lighting them?"

Taking another sip from her glass, Caroline paused thoughtfully. "I will."

She closed her eyes for a moment before all the black candles burst to life. A silver line formed between each candle, forming a silver circle around the pair.

Caroline opened her eyes and frowned. "Why does it look like we just cast a circle for spell casting?"

"We did."

She laughed. "What? I thought we came to see the stars?"

Erick stood and looked down at her. He wasn't smiling. "You can see the stars, but tonight will be the last time that will happen."

Her heart raced. Was this a joke? "Erick! What is this? You're scaring me." She pulled the blankets tighter around her body, watching him.

"You are here to give me your family's power." He crossed his arms and sneered at her.

Caroline gasped loudly as she stared up at him. He towered over her from where she remained on the ground. "This was all a trick? I trusted you!"

"It really was all too easy. Didn't you hear what happened to Sandy?" He rolled his eyes. "Of course not. Because you, like everyone else, were too busy with the ball. I did something similar. You are all so naive. Not one of you have half a brain. Really, more like child's play, Caroline."

"How dare you!"

Erick rocked back his head and laughed.

"No! You are not taking it. I'm not easy prey. I'm more powerful than you realize."

Erick sneered down at her as she glared up at him in return.

"I planned for a more difficult situation. The wine was laced with a sedative. You should be feeling it soon. It will knock you out and then I will complete the ritual. I know to move your body rather than leave it in the woods like I did Sandy's. They will think you ran away."

Caroline wobbled but managed to stand. The blankets fell around her as she raised her hands before her. They began to glow with silver-white light, and Erick frowned.

"I see. This will be a challenge, then." Erick lifted his hands and gold and black smoke swirled around him. He pushed his arm forward, and the smoke rushed toward Caroline.

Caroline screamed as his magic hit her. Her power exploded out of her body in response. Lightning lit up the clearing and the circle around the two began to glow white.

Erick glanced around him. He continued to pour magic from his hands as Caroline began to glow like a star before him.

Snow lifted around them within the circle of candles and the ground started to shake.

"What is happening? What have you done?" Erick screamed, but Caroline remained silent.

She gritted her teeth, channeling more power into the circle, burning through the haze the doctored wine caused.

Erick flicked his gaze to Caroline's eyes. They glowed

bright white. The earth beneath him shuddered differently, and then Caroline exploded like a supernova. White-hot power rushed toward Erick, knocking him to the ground before encompassing everything around them.

The circle filled with silver fire before a loud pop filled the air. The light in the middle disintegrated the circle, letting power escape into the air around it, and soon all that was left where the couple stood were two piles of smoldering ash.

Light blinked around her as she slowly opened her eyes. Caroline yawned and tried to stretch. Her body felt strange — like she was floating on something. Water? Air? Whatever it was, it was warm. She tried to roll unsuccessfully and looked down at herself to figure out why, only to discover she was nothing but bright light. Her body was a wisp of what looked like clouds. Was she now a ghost? What happened?

She glanced around her and observed that she hovered above the earth. Its blue and green surface glimmered below. With a blink, her magic stirred and she was able to zoom in. Her heart ached and her vision changed again as she viewed a campus decorated for Christmas.

Lights danced and candles hovered in the air, but the campus seemed off. It was quiet, and students were out in an unusually large number. Something tugged at her heart, like a voice calling to her from somewhere, and she blinked once again.

Her vision changed, and she now saw her family gathered before a large group of people lighting candles. Other families stood nearby. Each of them wore a solemn expression.

"I see you're awake, youngling." Caroline turned her head, and an older woman wearing a glowing white robe stood before her.

"Who are you?"

"I am your great, great, great grandmother Lola. I too

unleashed all my magic at once to save our family and ended up here. Before long, you too will have the ability to move around. I'll teach you."

"So you mean to say that I'm dead?" Caroline gasped.

"In a way, dear, you are, but not completely. You will neither move on from here or return to life below. You have joined our family line here in the stars to watch over our lineage until we are needed someday." Lola smiled confidently.

Tears leaked from Caroline's eyes. "Do I have a choice in that?"

"You don't, dear, but you will come to like this existence. We all have. Now, I recommend that you give it time before you check in on your family again. It will be a difficult adjustment for a while. I know you can do it. You are, after all, a Stars child, and we lend our power to those in need when called. It helps if they have a connection with the stars and even more so when it's family."

Caroline took a deep breath and recalled her magic. "I guess I'll do what I must. What if those who ask for our help intend to harm another?"

"We can decide whether to help them or not, my dear. We can sense the will of their heart when they ask."

"Then our power and assistance can't be abused?"

"Correct, sweet Caroline. Now you need to rest and let yourself adjust." Lola smiled before fading away.

"Thank you," Caroline whispered. With a sigh, she closed her eyes and fell into a deep sleep.

MADILYNN DALE

Award-winning and best-selling author Madilynn Dale writes stories that draw readers in and leaves them begging for more.

Originating from rural Oklahoma, her days are filled with love, family, work, and writing. Her creative inspiration is filled by nature, akin to the forest she grew up around.

Her best-selling work, The Fae Shifters Omnibus, gives readers a glimpse into her early foray into writing.

The award-winning novel Black Flames shares the evolution of her writing, having received multiple awards through the BookFest. With many stories on the horizon, you'll find Mrs. Dale scribbling away in one of her many notebooks and sipping on a coffee.

Check out more about this fabulous author at her website:

www.thechaptergoddess.com

facebook.com/MadilynnDaleAuthor

instagram.com/madilynndalewrites

tiktok.com/@mdwriter

THE MATTER OF WORDOL AND BURBOGH

JOSHUA A. BROWN

The urn sailed through the air, smashing against the stone wall. Pieces of the fine pottery scattered, and the ashes that had been inside billowed out in a thick, gray cloud. There was a low yelp from within the billowing cloud, followed by skittering sounds. A barely visible figure stepped forward to examine the calamity. The cloud from the ashes had begun to settle, and the person staring into it narrowed her eyes. Her quarry wasn't there.

Princess Mariella was wide-eyed, scowling, and brandishing a large, slightly bent pole axe with white-knuckled hands. She had directed the enormous weapon toward where the urn had been cast, and now, panting, she regarded that once again, the small, dreadful thing had disappeared. There was a noise behind her, but as she spun toward it with the pole axe, emitting a high-pitched cry, her eyes came to rest on an entourage of people—the surliest of which was her father, King Walan.

"What is the meaning of this?" he demanded as he looked around the chamber. A tapestry clung to the wall by a few threads. There were numerous items—priceless items—which were now small, decorative piles of rubble. A small fire burned at one end of the room and sticking out of it was the remnants of a painting—a painting of the king no less, with his then-younger, smiling daughter.

"Father," she said flatly, letting the pole axe fall to the floor with a clang. "We're under attack, and it's threatening the holiday celebration."

"The holiday?" a nobleman asked over the shoulder of the king.

"The winter solstice," she answered as her eyes began to sparkle. The man and the king exchanged a glance with furrowed brows, and the king drew in a long breath.

"Attack…from what?" he asked.

"It has no name," she replied, turning her attention to her father. "A fearsome beast marauding its deadly way through our castle, threatening to ruin all we have done to prepare for the holiday."

"Must you?" the king asked.

"I must!" Mariella snapped. The king's mouth fell open, but instead, he shook his head.

"I want this cleaned up, and all of these treasures will be paid for out of your inheritance!" he bellowed at her, at which time she immediately began to sob.

"But what of this monster?" she wept.

"If by 'monster' you mean that scaly little ball that has been knocking a few things over and urinating in water troughs, then I will take care of that," the king growled. "For I know exactly where it came from and who sent it."

"But we must get rid of it now!" She stomped her feet. "We must have the celebration! We already had our gaiety and the musical number."

"Yes…" the king uttered. "I'm still not sure the forest animals have quite recovered."

"Then you must put a stop to it!" she sobbed. "How can I be surprised by the gifts from my most loyal friends if there is no celebration?"

"The surprise is that they still remain friends with you," the king muttered under his breath. "Now have this cleaned up, and I will investigate this creature."

But before either of them could move, the towering doors to the chamber were thrown open, swinging with such force that when they hit the walls to either side of the door's frame, it sounded like cannons going off. Horns sounded a fanfare, and in strode a picture of such magnificence, a gasp surged through the room. The king's assistant—Rogerous—leaned completely over the king's shoulder from behind and pointed.

"The bishop!" he blurted.

But as the bishop—Landus, by name—further entered the chamber, he came to a halt, and the king elbowed Rogerous to remind him how close he was standing.

The king acknowledged the bishop with a single nod.

The bishop returned the nod, and then extended his ring-covered fingers outward as a number of the king's entourage raced forward to begin kissing both of the bejeweled hands. The bishop sighed as they did so, then shifted his gaze at the king.

The bishop was—or had been—a very handsome man. He was now a man of much distinction, a well-aged, noble religious figure who was always ready to advise the king from the viewpoint of god. He smirked as he looked around the room briefly, and then his eyes fell on Mariella, who gave a deep curtsey and smiled at him.

"I came as soon as I heard," the bishop proclaimed boldly. The king's brow wrinkled.

"Heard what?" he asked.

"That within these walls…" the bishop said, gesturing and letting his hand wave around a bit. "There lurks a monster!"

"Well…" the king uttered. "I wouldn't be in too much of a rush to invoke your holy powers. I was just about to inquire about such a thing from the wizard who likely created it."

"You don't mean…?" the bishop stammered.

"Yes, I'm afraid I must go to the Tower of Allundok and seek out the wizard, Wordol the Perturbator."

Another gasp ran through the room.

"If you must go, then go with god..." the bishop announced, stepping forward to put a hand on King Walan's shoulder.

"Then you're coming with me?" Walan asked.

"Oh, heavens no," the bishop said quickly. "These robes are too sensitive for such a dusty place."

"But...god," Walan said, raising an eyebrow.

"In such a dangerous place, I would recommend that you take with you the greatest of your knights," the bishop suggested. "Sir Holliver Tandworth!"

The delighted sigh that flowed from Mariella drew King Walan's attention and ire in a flash, and he turned toward his daughter.

"Oh, stop that!" he squawked at her, which brought forth a disgusted expression, and she stuck her tongue out at him.

"Someone needs my assistance?" Sir Holliver seemed to appear from nowhere near the king. His flowing blonde locks came to a halt after he did, and his strong chin was a thing of beauty. His eyes of deep blue sparkled with charm as he stood in his shiny, well-polished suit of armor.

Walan rolled his eyes while Mariella batted hers, and the bishop rubbed a finger along the side of his nose, directing it toward Sir Holliver like some sort of salute. Holliver directed it right back at the flowing, ornate cleric.

"I suppose so," Walan muttered reluctantly. "I am to journey to the Tower of Allundok, to take an audience with the wizard Wordol. You will accompany me."

"Very well," Holliver said in a low and commanding tone, which caused Mariella to clutch her chest, gulping out an adoring yelp. "I shall assemble archers...men-at-arms...squires ... We will bring this foul sorcerer to his kneeees..."

"Perhaps we'll go first and just have a word with him, you

and I," Walan said. Holliver stood back a bit and lifted his chin.

"As you wish, my liege," he said.

"Rogerous," Walan said. "Prepare horses. We ride at once."

"Right away, your majesty!" Rogerous said, and hurried away.

The Tower of Allunduk was a grim and somber place, a spire of stone reaching from the bottom of a basin to more than a hundred feet above the rocky hills. From the tower, one could—if so inclined—look out one of its windows out over the wide, lush valley below where much of the kingdom's largest city spread. In the center of the city was the great castle where Walan reigned, and as it turned out, imposed his thoroughly unfair will upon its subjects.

One of the subjects in question was morose, slouched on a grand chair in the tower's audience chamber, which doubled as a workshop. This gloomy individual was draped in robes of purple, leaning so that his head had come to rest on his left hand, and after a moment, he drew in a long breath, causing his shoulders to rise. He let go of it as a mighty sigh—the fourth such sigh in as many minutes—which caused an irritable shift from something else nearby.

He was the mighty wizard Wordol. And though he considered himself Wordol the Wise, Wordol the Conflagrator, Wordol the Scourge, the Storm Bringer, and many other names, he had become known to all others who cared of such things as "Wordol the Perturbator," as his magic wasn't so much devastating as it was...annoying. He was around the king's age, with a long, lean face and a head of long, gray hair. Now, at the sound of the shifting shape near him, he looked over.

There his eyes fell upon a scaled beast, lizard-like with a ridge of spines down its back, and a tail that ended in a pointed barb. This dragon was Maraxol and was roughly the size of a cow as it remained on a perch which had been built for it.

Wordol knew the dragon's expression, and he straightened on his chair at the sight of it. The dragon, ever present in the tower, cocked its head to the side as Wordol's expression flattened.

"And what was that for?" Wordol asked.

"You know very well," Maraxol answered, and then mocked his sigh. "If you are so exasperated at this, perhaps you should do something about it."

"I live...abandoned," Wordol said dramatically. "In exile, I am left to remain here until I find the mercy of death."

The dragon's dark eyes rolled.

"Oh, good gracious..." it groaned. "You missed your vocation. Perhaps you belong upon the stage, for all of the dramatic inclinations you possess."

"You mock me?" Wordol asked.

"I do," the dragon replied and smiled. A big smile. A toothy grin, during which a small trail of steamy smoke escaped in a tendril from between two teeth.

"I have begun to seek my vengeance," Wordol grumbled and folded his arms across his chest. A rumble of laughter came from the dragon. Briefly, its forked tongue slid across its lips.

"Your little, ugly ball of mischief is hardly vengeance," Maraxol said.

"What then?" Wordol asked. "A curse upon his kin? Blight upon the entirety of his kingdom's crops and livestock?"

"Or perhaps, you could go and implore him," the dragon suggested. "There is no need for your theatrics. You will only make things worse. Especially considering that it is nearing the time of the holiday for you two-legged monstrosities."

There was a gasping sound and other sounds as Wordol's amazed and shocked expression was paired with his seeming inability to form words. Finally, he rose from his chair, and his hands went to his hips. Wordol's face twitched, and it had turned—to Maraxol—a very odd shade of red. But in all of this, the dragon merely found all of this to be amusing. Adorable. Maraxol flexed his claws, and then settled down further on the perch.

"But one thing I can never figure out," Maraxol said, glancing around the chamber. "This holiday... What is it all about?"

"I'm not talking to you!" Wordol blurted. "I will save my next words for the king!" And with that, Wordol stormed from the chamber.

The dragon sighed. "Thank goodness. Now I can finally nap."

But the dragon couldn't nap because of the mighty pounding that came to the door a short while later, causing one of Maraxol's eyes to open. Brow lowered, and the dragon wondered if Wordol had—once again—forgotten to take his key for the tower's mighty door.

No matter, the hunchback could open the door for him, which would allow them to make their way inside. And if the dragon was lucky, he could get at least ten more minutes of respite from the wizard and his whining. A thought then occurred to the dragon—had it actually been long enough for Wordol to have gone to the castle and returned? Maraxol's neck straightened, and the dragon shifted on its perch.

Meanwhile, in the castle, under the direction of Mariella, the chamber had been cleaned and straightened, and it looked very proper again. She smiled, and then thought of her brave, noble Holliver making the journey with the king to root out the source of this evil that had infested the castle. She sighed with delight at the thought of the tall, brave, fit—very fit—knight, who seemed not to notice her sometimes. Of course, that was likely just him, as a servant of the king and kingdom, not wishing to be improper.

She took one last look at the chamber before heading down a corridor toward the throne room. There, she could at least order some people around while she waited for her father, and the wonderful, strong Holliver to return, informing her that the evil was gone and that the holiday could go on as it should. The musical celebration had been very magical, as it always was for her. It was likely special for the subjects of the kingdom and the many animals from the farms and forests as well. They seemed to disappear every year afterward, probably to spread the word that the princess had blessed the holiday.

She entered the throne room, and no sooner had she done so than had horns had sounded, and one of the pages rose from where he sat to point.

"The bishop!" he exclaimed, creating a stir and a gasp in the room. Presently, the bishop appeared and halted just inside the room to lift a hand toward the assembly.

"Your Holiness," Mariella said, sounding bored.

"Your Highness," he responded, sounding haughty.

Then they both halted and stared. They heard a growl, and suddenly it was there, right in front of the both of them on the dais where the thrones rested. Both had fixed their gazes on it, but while the bishop's expression was cautious, even somewhat fearful, the princess's twisted into a scowl. The thing. The evil.

"You…" she snarled, bringing up a shaking finger to point at it.

It was small, perhaps about the size of a human adult's head. It appeared perpetually hunched, and had large, black, adorable eyes. The mouth was a sort of wicked grin with sharp, pointed teeth, and the arms it had were tipped with little claws. It had a stub of a tail, and presently, under the glare of the princess and the stare of the bishop, its mouth fell open, and its tongue drooped out.

"Awwww!" came the collective sound from the people in the throne room. But a violent wave of the princess's hand silenced them, and she closed in on the evil.

"I'll put a stop to you…" she warned.

"My lady!" the bishop warned.

The creature leapt upward as she lunged for it, and it came

to light on a large, ornate tapestry behind the thrones. It extended a claw, looking at her as her eyes became wild.

"You wouldn't dare!" she bellowed at it. The thing chattered with laughter.

"Guards!" she roared. "Spear that thing!"

The guards moved and the little beast stuck a claw in the tapestry and slid downward, slicing the length of it as it headed to the floor. By the time it plopped onto the stone, she had snatched up a torch, and she dove for it again. It made a cute and sudden noise as it rolled away, but before she knew what was happening, to her horror, Mariella had ignited the tapestry, and it was quickly ablaze.

"Oh..." the bishop groaned. "And I liked that one so much." Mariella's hardened gaze darted back to him. The creature was gone.

Walan and Holliver cautiously made their way into and up the tower, accompanied by Nurch, the hunchbacked butler of the tower. But while the tower's lone servant carried on at length, the king and his bold knight followed along, periodically exchanging glances and rolling their eyes. Their business was with the tower's master, and they had little time or interest in anything else. Finally, the knight decided to end the ramblings about the root cellar by inquiring with the king.

"Who is the master of this place?" Holliver asked.

"Of course you know of Wordol, the wizard," Walan replied.

"I do, and his dark sorcery throughout the kingdom... A foul and vile practitioner of the most sinister magic. We should—"

"Well, clearly you've heard of him," Walan uttered, casting a glance at the knight. "His magical abilities cause more irritation than tragedy."

"Oh," the knight said. "And is it that he hates the holiday? Is that why he has attacked us?"

"Hate the holiday?" the king asked. "Who could hate the holiday?"

"What holiday does he hate?" Nurch asked.

"Silence, servant," Tolliver ordered as they approached the door. "Open the door, and announce us to your master."

"Very well, Sir Knight," Nurch acknowledged and thumped on the door three times. "In you go."

Nurch opened the tall door, revealing the inside of the audience chamber, which both visitors looked at. They entered cautiously, taking note of the various bookshelves, the empty chair, and the many tables and benches where magical work was conducted. Walan took it all in with wonder, never having seen any of it. Tolliver's hand was on his sword as they made their way further into the room, while Nurch had given a bow and hurried away. Soon enough, the pair were in the center of the room and came to a pause. Holliver shrugged.

"He is gone," the knight said.

"Yes," the king acknowledged. "But to where?"

"I know where he's gone..." Maraxol said from the perch. Both men hopped and leapt around, looking for the source of the voice. Finally, they came to look at the perch, and the king's eyes widened.

"Good heavens! A dragon!" he blurted.

A shriek escaped Holliver, which prompted a glance between the dragon and the king. Finally, Holliver straightened himself and cleared his throat.

"Well, of course, as royal knight, it is my duty to slay such a beast," he proclaimed, prompting a growl from the dragon.

"It's been a long time since I've partaken of roasted knight," Maraxol warned. Holliver swallowed a nervous lump and smiled at the dragon.

"You, uh...said you knew where your master had gone," Walan said.

The dragon laughed.

"Master?" it asked. "Wordol?"

"He is not your master?" the king asked.

"Hardly," Maraxol said. "But I know he's gone to the castle."

"Good lord, sire!" Holliver burst in dramatic fashion. "He'll burn them all!"

"I suppose I should help this come to a close," the dragon sighed. "Very well, come forth, and simply touch my scales."

King Walan and Holliver exchanged a glance.

Meanwhile, an enormous plume of purple fire erupted in the center of the already-smoking throne room. Presently, from inside the plume, there came a series of yelps, and Wordol hopped from the fire as it trailed away. Several small fires burned on his robes, but he was quick to swat them out. As he finally came to a rest to straighten his smoking robes, he looked up and into the points of twenty spears and just as many bows. He let his eyes dart back and forth across them.

"Are you not terrified?" he asked.

The guards didn't move.

"Your entrance does lack a certain level of horror when the person most in danger is…you," the bishop said from near the throne.

"Well, I have come to…" Wordol said, and then gently reached out to move a spear from in front of his face. "…to exact my revenge for the affront to me."

"I can't think of why anyone would not want you around," Mariella said. "Are you to thank for the terrible little goblin running about this castle?"

"Burbogh?" Wordol asked and gave as sinister a laugh as he could manage. "Yes, he is one of my curses upon you."

Presently, little Burbogh waddled into view and was quick

to skitter to Wordol's side, cooing as the wizard looked down, then up at the princess.

"So…" the bishop said, looking rather annoyed. "What is it you want?"

But there was a red flash in the room, and to a chorus of cries and screams, the dragon Maraxol appeared. The cries and screams turned to gasps and murmurs as the king and Holliver were spotted with the dragon. Mariella was off her throne in an instant, but the bishop had prevented her from racing down to meet her father.

"Holliver!" she cried. He smiled his amazingly charming smile and gave her a deep bow.

"Your Majesty!" the bishop blurted. "Stand back, and I shall smite this dragon at once!"

"Stay your smiting," Walan commanded and shifted his gaze to the wizard. "Hello Wordol… Brother."

"Your communing with my dragon is too late!" Wordol burst, whipping his left hand upward.

"See?" the dragon uttered quietly from behind the king. "Dramatics."

"Since he was a boy…" King Walan agreed.

"I have come to finally exact my revenge!" Wordol announced. "For your transgression some three days ago. You dare to exile me?"

Now, Walan's face wrinkled. Mariella and the bishop exchanged a glance, while Holliver did his best not to look confused.

"Exiled." Walan said flatly. "You…dolt."

"And right before the holiday," Wordol added.

"I was speaking on the holiday," Walan said. "The winter solstice holiday is a glorious time of year, and it is a time when we give, and we love a little more."

He had placed his hands over his heart.

"And we sing!" Mariella said, extending her arms to the sides as the royal musicians began to play a sweeping melody.

A single, swiftly-raised hand from King Walan restored silence to the throne room.

Mariella growled and stomped her foot. "You never let me have any fun!" she raged at him. She hurled herself down to her throne and angrily folded her arms across her chest. The dragon leaned toward Holliver with a grin on its dragony face.

"Oh, I *like* her…" it whispered. Holliver smiled nervously.

"So, to celebrate the winter solstice—the time of this holy blessing
from god of the promise of another year," Wordol sneered, "you choose to exile me?"

"I did not exile you!" Walan shouted.

"You said: 'And as we all recover from another musical episode of the princess, we celebrate this exiled wizard,' and you indicated *me* in that town square!" Wordol recalled.

"You…infernal idiot," Walan said with a shake of his head. "This is why I was made king and you were sent off with the witch to learn your craft. I said 'celebrate this exalted wizard.'"

There was silence. Steely silence. Petrifying, mortifying silence. Wordol shuffled his feet, and then glanced at the dragon. Maraxol shook its mighty head slowly while Holliver gave a shrug.

"Well…" Wordol said. "I suppose, then, it is time I…take my leave."

"Wordol," Walan said and smiled. "How about you stay for the holiday dinner?"

Wordol thought for a moment, and then smiled. "I accept," he said. "Provided my dragon and Burbogh are also welcome."

"Yes…" Walan muttered, looking at the dragon, and then at the little…thing …beside his brother. "That will be fine."

"Not the monster!" Mariella shrieked, leaving her throne again. She had come forward to glare at it, but found it already looking at her. Looking with eyes big, black, and bulbous that froze her, its little mouth quivered. She paused, really looking at it, and at once, she shifted her gaze to the king. "I suppose, in the name of the holiday...it would be all right."

"The holiday?" the bishop asked.

"Exactly," the king said.

"To the dining halls!" Rogerous said from behind the thrones. "We feast!"

The holiday was safe.

Peace had been restored, and it was time to eat.

JOSHUA A. BROWN

Joshua A. Brown is a child of the blockbuster era of films. His imagination was stoked by exposure to many works of literature, film, and music from an early age. A former police officer, Joshua is now a musician, filmmaker and published author.

He lives in the country in central Iowa and is a graduate of Iowa State University.

For more information on Josh and his many projects, check out:

www.facebook.com/groups/wolfshirebooksjb

PLAYING WITH STARLIGHT
MICHELLE CROW

How could this have happened? How could she, Clarity Clearwater, the least qualified student in Spellmouth High's theater class, be cast as the lead character for the upcoming Yule play?

Clarity glared at the piece of paper pinned to the corkboard, her lavender eyes tracing the lines and curves of her name. Not only was she not qualified, but she hadn't even tried out. She didn't know how to lead anything. And who would follow her? Sure, she could just charm them with her charisma magic. That's how she got into the class to begin with. All she'd hoped for was a background character or to work behind the scenes—not lead!

"See, I told you you were up there," Harley, her best and only friend, said.

Clarity just stared at the paper as her stomach tightened along with her chest.

A locker banged shut behind her, followed by a honey-combed voice that could only belong to Stormy Nix. "You know you're going to bungle the whole production, right?"

Clarity tore her gaze from the paper. Students lined the halls by their lockers, broken out into groups of two or more.

The ones closest to them stopped chatting to listen and watch. Anticipation thickened the air around them.

Stormy crossed the hall and glared down at Clarity. She was, and always had been, a head taller. "How did you do it?" she demanded. More of the small groups clustered closer.

"Do what?" Clarity asked, heart pounding.

Stormy rolled her cerulean eyes and huffed. Not a single hair fell free from her bright-blonde top bun, and Clarity wondered if the girl even knew how to let her hair down. "Get the part, idiot."

"I—" she started to reply but was cut off by Stormy jabbing a finger in her chest.

"I'm going to find out how you stole the part and demand that Mrs. Jones make me the rightful lead."

Harley smacked Stormy's finger from Clarity's chest and pushed the girl back. "Back off, Stormy. Not like your name was even on the board."

Stormy never took her eyes off Clarity, ignoring Harley's disruption. "I'll just have to remind Mrs. Jones of the performance you put on during 4th year."

Clarity's cheeks burned at the memory. Someone laughed behind them, and she was certain they remembered it too. She hadn't wanted that part either. She'd tried out for the role of some side character, a non-speaking part. But her stupid powers always seemed to get her placed at the top. No matter what, she was always picked first, always placed in the top three—if not first in sports—and always got straight A's. It was boring and lonely at the top for a Charisma Witch. And so, she protested the 4th year play and found herself in detention for two weeks after. Which only lasted the first hour before her Charisma had her freed from detention.

"I didn't even try out, Stormy. I'll happily go tell Mrs. Jones to replace me. You were born for this crap anyway."

Stormy balled her hands into fists at her sides. "So you don't think I can get it on my own, huh?"

Harley's eyes widened. "Oh, here we go."

"What?" Clarity shook her head. "No, I am saying I don't care. It's yours. You can have it."

Narrowing her eyes and furrowing her perfectly sculpted brows, Stormy leaned in close. Anyone watching—in other words, everyone—pulsed with excitement at the prospect of a fight. Even the buzzing fluorescent lights above seemed to spotlight only them. Clarity wished that for one second she couldn't feel others' emotions. Maybe then they'd just fade into the background against their lockers.

Harley made a sound and moved toward them, but Clarity stopped her with a hand. Stormy might be taller than her, but she would be crazy to even try anything against Clarity. Something blossomed across her smooth, pimple-free face. A look that twisted Clarity's gut in a different way than the unexpected casting. Stormy relaxed and leaned back, but the smile she trained on Clarity was unnerving. Without a word, she turned and walked away. The anticipation melted along with a disappointed sigh from several of their peers.

"What the hell was that all about?" Harley asked.

"Hell if I know. She has always hated me."

"Not always." Harley leaned against the locker. "You guys were best friends long before I came into the picture."

Clarity remembered... back when Stormy used to share her secrets with her and how they learned their first bit of spellcasting together. She also recalled when one particular spell went horribly wrong and her Charisma was cut off for a week. It was wonderful. Well, except for the part where her grades slipped, her spells failed, and Stormy decided from then on they would be mortal enemies. That last part was still confusing to Clarity, but after a while, she'd just settled into their friends-to-enemies routine.

"Whatever." The halls narrowed around her as she remembered the more pressing matter: play lead. It would be easier to walk out of school and never return. Then she wouldn't have to be a part of the stupid play or deal with Stormy. "I need to get out of this play. I can't be a lead. No way!"

"I think you should do it," Harley said.

"And I think you're bonkers," Clarity said, a small smile creeping back onto her face.

The bell rang, and any thoughts of fleeing left as the hall cleared of students heading to their next classes.

Mrs. Jones sat behind her desk with a soft smile. She wore a bright-pink hoodie with #theatermom in vibrant white across the chest.

"I've printed the casting list and already ordered the programs. I can't reconsider Miss Nix for the lead part. That's yours, Clarity."

"But I'm the worst possible choice."

"Why?"

Clarity paused, trying to pinpoint all the reasons why, but her mind was blank.

"See, even you know deep down you can do this."

"But I didn't even try out! And *you* remember what happened in the 4th year play. Everyone does," Clarity said.

Mrs. Jones's smile faltered for a moment but quickly returned. "Oh, nonsense. You were putting on your own show that evening. You know what I remember?"

"What?"

"A scared and sad little girl who didn't want to shine in the light because she didn't think she was good enough."

Clarity looked at her shoes, not wanting to meet Mrs. Jones's judgy gaze. Everyone knew her family's tragic story and how their lives ended that year.

Mrs. Jones stood up and came around to sit on the desk in front of Clarity. "You've been through a lot in just fifteen years, Clarity. It's okay to just feel for yourself sometimes. I know you do enough *feeling* for others already. Your powers are incredibly strong, just like hers were."

"*...just like hers were.*"

It had been years since the event, and it still hurt to remember. Yes, she'd acted out at the play because she didn't want to perform. But she also didn't want to have to deal with everyone else's pity—which smothered her when she entered a room, let alone a crowded theater.

"Then you know I could just Charisma you into replacing me for that role."

Mrs. Jones frowned. "You could try, but my wards are in place. You would have to undo those first, if you could find them, and translate the runes too. It's a tedious affair, and it would get us nowhere. This can be good for you, Clarity. I know you've been trying to fail on purpose this semester. You know you can talk to me. My door is always open."

Clarity didn't want to talk. She didn't want any of this. The attention and pity. It came pouring out of Mrs. Jones, reminding Clarity of what she'd lost. "I didn't know you were a counselor too, Mrs. Jones." She regretted it instantly as a touch of pain bubbled out of Mrs. Jones.

The theater teacher made her way back around her big, oak desk and sat down. She leaned on her elbows, steepling her fingers. "You will play the best Queen Moral that Spellmouth High has ever had in this year's Yule play. That's all for today, Miss Clearwater."

Two weeks and one day later, Clarity sat in front of the dressing room mirror as Harley applied a generous amount of glitter to her cheeks.

"This is so stupid," Clarity said.

Harley put the tube of glitter down and picked up an eyeliner pencil. "Stay still. You don't want me to shish kabob your eye now, do you?"

Clarity stared at the mirror as her friend made her up for the play. She'd tried three times and failed each time to get out of it. Even her dad backed up Mrs. Jones's casting decision and threatened her with a week of no after-school Hexing Club if she didn't comply.

"Maybe I do want you to run me through with that eyeliner. It would be better than being forced to act."

Harley put down the pencil and grabbed Clarity by the shoulders. "Don't do that!"

"Do what?"

"I can feel your magic too, you know. I felt the pull just then. You can't ever ask me or anyone else, especially anyone else, to hurt you. Who knows what might happen!"

Clarity sighed. She knew that if she pulled enough, anyone could be swayed to do her bidding. Some required more of a pull and others, just a niggle. At least Harley always called her out on it.

The play started with a bang, quite literally. One of the overhead lights burst, and sparks spewed from where the bulb shattered. A tangle of dread twisted out from the crowd of onlookers, slamming hard into Clarity as she watched from center stage. The audience jumped up and rushed for the exits as the sparks rained down, igniting tiny fires.

It didn't seem right. It didn't seem natural. None of the fleeing audience could get the doors to open, and their panic filled the air with a sharp, tinny flavor. Clarity searched for her dad in the crowd but couldn't make out anyone's face, just arms and legs in a sea of mashed-together forms. Mrs. Jones, came racing down the aisle with a fire extinguisher. She tried to put the flames out, but they burned an unnaturally bright green, and the extinguisher didn't do what it was meant to.

A flash on the catwalk caught Clarity's attention, and the

familiar sense of arrogance, laced with guilt and fear, greeted her. *Stormy.*

The girl was scrambling away from the catwalk with a brilliant glow in her hands. Its light seemed to dim and pulse.

Clarity strode over to the only place Stormy could flee from once she climbed down and glared at her. "What did you do?"

"I—I—" Stormy stuttered. All of her usual arrogance bled away, replaced with the sourness of guilt and regret.

"Stormy Skye Nix, what did you do!"

"I tried to cast a simple starlight hex to blind you for a few seconds when the spotlight hit your face. I thought seeing you fudge your lines would be funny, but it backfired."

"Starlight! You can't play with starlight! That's advanced practitioner stuff."

"I know! I don't know what to do!" The light still pulsed in her hands, which were pink and blistered. Some skin was already peeling away around her fingertips. She gasped for breath as her hands trembled.

Clarity looked around the theater and considered their situation. "I need to calm everyone down. Then we can see if anyone has a counter-spell for star fire."

"I'm so sorry, oh my god. I'm going to be freaking expelled for this!" Stormy said through a sob.

"Yeah, you probably will, assuming we don't die in here. Come on." Clarity climbed off the stage and placed her hands in a prayer pose at her chest. Her Charisma usually worked without any prompting, but for an entire theater room of panicked people, she'd need to crank up the juice a bit. Releasing the prayer hands, she waved her right hand through the air to draw a charm rune. Only the spellcaster could see the color of their magic, and hers was purple.

Taking a slow and steady breath, she pushed her calming energy out toward the crowd. Within seconds, they started to relax and step away from the exits—anxiety leaching away from them. Clarity snapped her fingers, and the crowd turned to face her.

"Does anyone know anything about starlight or star magic? Anything to put out star fire?"

"I can try," someone said, stepping away from the crowd.

"Good. Now, why the hell are the doors locked?"

Stormy cleared her throat behind Clarity. "I might have woven a locking spell on them, but I can't undo it with my hands all burnt."

Clarity inhaled slowly and pushed her anger aside for now. "Anyone know any spells of unlocking?"

"I do," another voice said from the crowd—a woman wearing a rich blue-and-white checkered scarf.

"Can you please work on opening those doors? Everyone else, give them room." On command, the entire crowd opened a path to the doors.

"What do you want me to do, Clarity?" Harley asked from the stage. The entire stage crew fanned out behind her, their eyes darting around at the chaos.

"While they work to unlock the front doors, can you start guiding people out the back exits in calm, orderly lines?"

Harley gave her a thumbs up and then whistled to her crew. "You heard her, let's get these people to safety. One line down that aisle; one down that one," she said, pointing as she spoke.

"I'm so proud of you, kid."

Clarity spun around to find her father by her side. "Dad!"

"See, you're a *stellar* leader. Everyone was in crisis mode, but not you. You jumped right into chaos cleanup," he said, eyes warm and proud.

Scrunching up her nose, she shook her head. "No, Dad. No puns right now!"

· · ·

Two hours later, the star fire was extinguished, and everyone was evacuated onto the front lawn of Spellmouth High.

Stormy approached Clarity, head low. Mrs. Jones stood behind her, disappointment oozing off the theater teacher in torrents.

"I'm sorry for what I did, Clarity. It was so stupid and dangerous."

Clarity looked up at the girl and shook her head. "I can't say it's okay. But I think you already know just how bad this is."

Stormy nodded.

"What happened to us? Why do you hate me so much?"

Stormy raised her head, and watery blue eyes met Clarity's lavender. "I don't hate you. You just always get everything you want. You don't even have to try."

Not everything, she thought. She couldn't get her mother back. No amount of charm or Charisma could bring her back. "It's not exactly something I asked for, Stormy. I can't turn my magic off like others...use it only when I want to. It just happens."

Stormy's brows bunched as she considered that, perhaps for the first time. She looked away in shame and then walked slowly with Mrs. Jones toward her parents, who also seethed with disappointment and anger.

Harley bounded over and nudged Clarity with an elbow. "Dude, you led us out of there with a boss-level attitude," she said.

Clarity felt her cheeks warm at the compliment and attention. "Whatever. Someone had to calm the crowd. Nobody was using their brains."

Clarity smiled and looked to the night sky. Stars blanketed the sea of black, and Clarity realized something about herself. She could lead. Her magic didn't have to be such a burden after all... And maybe sometimes—in very small doses!—she kind of did like the attention.

MICHELLE CROW

Bestselling author Michelle Crow writes sci-fi fantasy, speculative fiction, and sometimes romance. She loves all things sci-fi, fantasy, humorous, or dystopian, and can often be found hiding away on the couch watching zombies take over the world or reading a new book while her ever-growing TBR pile winges from the corner.

Michelle, her husband, and their three monsters are currently traveling full-time in an RV looking for their next landing zone.

facebook.com/michellecrow.author

instagram.com/tabularasa_bea

amazon.com/stores/Michelle-Crow/author/B07QF1BHL7

Acknowledgments

Our little team is bursting with creative energy. This is our fifth anthology, and it's still just as exciting to work on as our very first.

We always start with an idea.

Then we write. And when we share our stories with one another, we are amazed at how very different one theme can evolve into different directions.

A huge shout out to this year's team:

B Crow

M.J.J. Mori

A. A. Warne

Adryanna Monteiro

Thank you. This book shines because of your dedication, support, expertise and amazing creative encouragement.

Also By

Book 1

A Fantasy Christmas: Tales by the Hearth

Book 2

The Magic in Fire

Book 3

When Sleeping Giants Wake

Book 4

Deals in Blood

www.ingramcontent.com/pod-product-compliance
Lightning Source LLC
Chambersburg PA
CBHW020138180626
46810CB00004B/1619